Farewell Route 66

Michael Lund

BeachhouseBooks

Saint Charles Missouri USA

ISBN 978-1-59630-108-5

Library of Congress Control Number: 2017947416

BeachHouse Books

www.beachhousebooks.com

an Imprint of

Science & Humanities Press

Saint Charles MO 63301

At Home and Away

by Michael Lund

This five-volume novel series chronicles an American family during times of peace and war from 1915 to 2015. The first book, *Route 66 Sweetheart*, is set mostly in and around Rutherford, New Jersey, during the 1930s. *Route 66 Dreamer* features the son of a Swedish immigrant who pursues his dreams of American success in Kansas and Missouri in the early 1940s. However, in both books some family members move away to distant countries and unexpected challenges.

The third volume, *Route 66 Looking-glass*, takes place primarily in Missouri in the mid-1960s, but characters also travel far from home and familiar experiences. *Farewell, Route 66* follows another generation of family members, this time from Missouri to Southeast Asia where many learn, sadly, "how to not tell a war story." In the final volume of the series, *Route 66 Redux*, the next generation travels to Europe and the Middle East to understand their identity in a multi-national community.

Farewell, Route 66

Michael Lund

2017

The Lindblooms
Oscar -m- Marian (Mid) Lacy
Louis -m- Suzanne McGovern
Curtis -m- Anne Carter
Carol -m- Mark Gonzáles
Benjamin -m- Elizabeth Stafford   Ethel   Sam   Lucy
Justin   Carl   Mary   Anne
Marian   Christie

Acknowledgments

The title of this book might suggest that I'm saying goodbye to the central subject of my fiction. That is not the case. A fifth and final book in this At Home and Away novel series is in progress because, like the rebirth of the Mother Road as "Historic Route 66," the story of America is always adding new chapters connected to its past.

I remain profoundly grateful to Dr. Bud Banis, publisher of BeachHouse Books, for his support of this saga and of me as an author.

I wish to thank my wife for careful proofreading and wise editorial suggestions, my son for the striking art of this book's cover, and my friends and family members for reading.

Portions of this work have appeared in different forms in the following venues. We are grateful for permission to reprint. "The Soy Bean Field," *Outside-In Literary and Travel Magazine*, Issue Fifteen (Fall, 2013) and in *Eating With Veterans* (BeachHouse Books, 2015); "Travelers," Military Experience and the Arts (May 19, 2014) http://militaryexperience.org/?s=Travelers; "Look-a-Like" and "Rules of Engagement" in *Eating With Veterans* (BeachHouse Books, 2015).

Prologue: Interchanges

"You know where Interstates 44 and 270 come together west of St. Louis?" I asked my son Curtis the day after my 98th birthday.

"Of course," he said. "We used to go through there all the time to see you and Dad in Fairfield. And even now, when we visit we can pass that way. Still a lot of traffic, especially at rush hour. People going into the city or around to Memphis or Chicago."

"Right. The goal of that construction was to remove bottlenecks and get people where they wanted to be faster and easier. But has it ever occurred to you that the cloverleaf itself is no one's destination? It's emptiness, a void."

"I've never thought about that! But we have dotted the country with these interchanges."

"It all started with the development of the Interstate system, replacing old two-lane roads with limited-access, four- or-more-lane highways. And that required more complex junctions. When you were growing up in Fairfield, road crossings were governed by stop sign and traffic lights. In most of those old fashioned intersections, you saw your fellow travelers coming and going. They were in the lane next to you, their faces smiling or scowling out the windows."

"Whereas now everyone going in one direction is separated from traffic going in other directions. And we're going much too fast to have a view of those behind or those ahead of us."

"That's what I'm thinking. The goal of these giant exchanges is to bring people together. But while gathering us, they also push us apart. All over the nation drivers and passengers are being spread out by these fields that possess nothing but space. No one lives in them; they have no businesses; even agriculturally they accomplish nothing but to create emptiness to be passed through."

"Interesting. I might have a counter to this complaint in my car. Be right back."

I had no idea what he would bring, though I feared it would be electronic--his little computer or one of those navigation devices people use now instead of maps. One of the grandchildren, little Marian who's in California now, showed me satellite pictures of places all over the world. She could even look at Fairfield, where Oscar and I lived for almost fifty years, and zoom in to the neighborhood where our children grew up.

While waiting, I looked out at the North Carolina river and the distant highway bridge reaching over half a mile from bank to bank. The late afternoon sun behind us slanted across the flat coastal farmland and, like a giant spotlight, lit up the span. On the way to evening its color would shift from its grey-brown to yellow to a rich orange.

On the way to my own evening, I wanted to linger in the dying light. As I prepared to narrate the next stage of the family history, I had less certitude about what it all means. The first parts were about events I came to understand after fifty years passed; but now the story resumes a mere twenty-some years ago, and history has not taken the clear shape hindsight usually grants. And the worst moment of my married life came at that time.

Yet I want to get this right for myself, my children, grandchildren, great-grandchildren. It used to be we had clear paths/roads we followed; but now we live in what the younger generation(s) term "cyberspace," a global

2

community that may soon even extend beyond to the moon or farther but which we can reach across in nanoseconds. Curtis has tagged this transition with the phrase, "Farewell, Route 66," and dealing with it is a struggle for us super seniors.

When he came in from the garage, he held something far more old-fashioned than a computer. "Are you going to measure a highway interchange with that carpenter's ruler?" I joked.

"I'm going to measure my whole life, the journey from age nine to however old I am today, from Missouri to here. You probably don't remember, but Grandpa gave Louis and me one of these carpenter's rulers one time when we visited him and Grandma." Carl and Sadie had lived in a little house with a cabinet shop in Jefferson City.

"That was nice. Of course, he wouldn't have given one to Carol; girls don't get tools."

"Correct, though it turns out you and your daughter, my sister, are the best builders and fixers in the family." He turned it about in his hand "Still, this came with a heavy weight."

"A heavy weight? Using it correctly?"

Curtis was unfolding the ruler, hinged in half-foot sections, its full length six feet.

"Not that. I was an impulsive kid, racing around and getting sudden inspirations--inspirations that should have been given a bit more reflection before being put into action."

"You didn't break yours, did you?"

"In less than 24 hours. I just loved unfolding it and refolding it, measuring stuff. I was already calibrating in the back seat before we got out of town and on the road home to Fairfield."

The drive was just about an hour in those days, a nice two-lane highway that wound around the Ozark foothills and crossed several rivers. Now, of course, the road is three- or four-lane and enters into many of those empty interchange spaces along its north/south route.

Curtis went on. "That darn Louis, of course, put his away so as never to break it. He always made me look bad."

"Now, now, sibling rivalries are supposed to fade as you grow older."

"I know. And, in fact, we're close. But it's fun to pretend. Anyway, there I was the next day with two sections of ruler, a jagged break separating them. What do do, what to do?"

"What *did* you do?"

"I hid them. Put them way back in a desk drawer covered up with papers. (Grandpa built that desk for me, so there's some irony here.) Anyway, I hoped there would never be an occasion to confess—especially to Dad—that I'd carelessly snapped in half this gift."

I laughed. "I doubt if your father ever thought about it, lost in the clouds as theoretical physicists tend to be. But what you're holding looks like it has no breaks in it. A replacement?"

"Nope the original. Here's what happened. That desk with all its contents stayed in Fairfield until I got to graduate school, when I carried it off to Atlanta. It's been with me since."

"So, the ruler was hidden in the same drawer for-- what? Twenty, thirty years?"

4

"Well, at least in the general area of the desk. I'd get one piece out of it now and then to measure something. I mean, it was still a ruler, after all. So, one or the other part of it would wander out to my shop or into another room, even into my car."

"Ah, a traveling ruler."

"One, in fact, that would travel through one of those interchanges you're complaining about, the one where I-95 and I-85 cross in Petersburg." He and Anne used to drive back and forth between Virginia and North Carolina until they moved full-time to this house on the water. I'm in a retirement community just twenty miles away now.

"I was digging around out in the garage recently and found one part of this." He held it up. "But then I remembered I had been using it in the house just the other day."

"You'd just carried it from the house to the garage."

"Not so. This was the other house. I don't know when they got separated, but, since I was always using just one, it didn't occur to me that sometimes it was this half," he pointed, "and sometimes this other. The numbering on one side of the ruler is reversed on the other: the mark for four feet is opposite the one for two feet; 48 inches above is 24 inches below. It might never occur to the person that he had one part today, a different one yesterday.

"So I got the two together and realized that its half-a-century jagged break was just the kind that could be glued, if it was well clamped." He handed it to me.

I could barely find the line where the two parts had been joined. "So, what I'm holding is the original ruler Grandpa gave you, restored and functional once again?"

"That's it. But it means much more to me. You see, an adult--even a senior--I've repaired a mistake I made as a child. I've joined the past and the present into one connected piece, a chronological continuum. I've also linked myself to my grandfather along the paternal line. There are empty spaces between us--highway cloverleafs, if you will--but this bridges those gaps."

I gave him back the ruler. "Hmm. In your hands is a tangible object that was once in his hands. When you remember that, you are connected to him. I like that! In fact, we may have to use that concept soon in the next section of the family saga you're transcribing for me. We have a lot of area to cover--from here in North Carolina back to St. Louis, over to Europe, into Southeast Asia, back through Iraq, and home to America's shores. We'll need all the bridges and overpasses and tunnels we can find to travel that distance."

"Tell you what." He put the repaired ruler into my purse. "Let's keep this with you, and when the stack of notes I'm taking is six inches high, we'll say we have covered enough ground for another volume. And those pages will connect the family, even though the generation of your grandchildren is spread around the globe more than we ever imagined they would be."

"Very good. In the meantime, let us beware of empty spaces we must cross."

Part 1: Oscar

Chapter I: Gathering

When their oldest son offered to host the Lindbloom family for a grand Christmas celebration that year (1990), Oscar and Mid were initially pleased. They knew he had the space; St. Louis was the most accessible central location; and in the last few years entertaining children and grandchildren over a several day period had begun to be for them as much a strain as a pleasure. They were, after all, into their eighth decade on the planet.

What they were less enthusiastic about was the proposal that grandparents, aunts, and uncles--that is, the older generations--should tell travel stories revealing something about themselves the others didn't know. "Truth or Dare" appealed to a reclusive Midwesterner and a woman from a self-reliant New England family even less than the established family game: Two-son Riddle. (Curtis was also that game's inventor, naming it after himself—his parents' second son—and linking it to one of his father's favorite bandleaders, Nelson Riddle.)

Their apprehension would prove justified, as the storytelling led to arguments about the nature of family. Some of their grandchildren took a stand that friends were their real family, and the entire clan wondered for a time if they would ever come together again.

"There will be prizes," Curtis wrote to his parents, to brother Louis and wife Suzanne, and to sister Carol and husband Mark. "The premise of Far Away/Close to Home is that experiences in travel often unexpectedly put the past in a new light."

Carol insisted, "All professional writers--Curtis, scholar; Louis, lawyer--begin with a ten point handicap. Me, I write code that you all can't read." She was a retired

8

Army technology specialist now working for a start-up computer company in the San Francisco area.

Curtis responded, "If we're handicapped, Dad would have to be penalized for his college radio dramas; and my wife has produced a lyrical botanical guide to the plants on granite outcrops in Central Virginia. So, let's just say content trumps style--which, in fact, it does."

At home in Fairfield Oscar told Mid, "We have time to prepare for this, choose an event, and dress it up with a bit of fiction, if we have to."

Retired for nearly a decade, Oscar had settled more and more into a routine while Mid lobbied for excursions to destinations close and distant. She said, "We could talk about our tour of Scandinavia. No one else has been there, so they can't dispute our account."

After he stopped teaching physics at South Central Missouri State University, Oscar had "survived" (his term) two overseas trips. One involved seven European countries in five days; the second took in Denmark, Sweden, and Norway over six days. Each whet Mid's appetite for adventure and discovery but strained her husband, who more and more was satisfied to just stay in the town where they'd lived for forty years.

"I suppose I could go back in time for a story, back to Kansas."

In the previous summer elder son Louis drove him to Salinas, where Oscar had grown up. They toured four small towns he'd lived in as his father moved from place to place, chasing construction jobs during the Depression. And in a nostalgic mood Oscar had recalled the struggles his parents endured and which he, their only child, only sensed at the time.

"Would it be fair to talk about a place you planned to visit?" Mid mused. "I'll describe my dream vacation on an island off the coast of Maine as if it has already happened."

"So long as you don't make me go there any time soon, I'll play along." He chuckled. Outsmarting his children did appeal to Oscar. "Wait! I will have been there with you, right?"

"Of course." Mid was already fashioning her tale. "You know, I believe I found an antique mantel clock in the little cottage we rented. Yes, there was a Seth Thomas. While you were building a glider in the old barn, I took the mechanism apart and went to work."

"I trust I stayed on the ground, especially as I seem to remember being very busy with a comely farmer's daughter who dropped by each day with fresh milk and butter."

"Not on your life. But there were a few visitors now and then, and we got involved in several local events. But right now, go practice your music, while I tinker with the cuckoo I got at Carnahan's and the story of an isolated lobster village on the Atlantic coast."

Oscar played saxophone with a little jazz combo, the Rockers of Age, made up of other retired professionals. He'd resumed a musical career twenty-five years ago that, Mid felt, saved him from a mid-life crisis. It may also have rescued her from depression.

Oscar had been burned out from teaching, battling for research money, dealing with growth strains in his department and the university. And then, Carol, their daughter, had shocked them by enlisting in the Army. Oscar and Mid recognized the extent of their anxiety

10

about her only when she came home a second and final time from Vietnam.

The boys were on steady paths at the time, Louis in law school and Curtis an English major at Westminster College. But the parents, rattling around the big house they'd just purchased, suffered from the empty nest syndrome. That's when A Woman's Hand, her antique clock restoration business, was born.

Their anxieties shifted over time to the fate of nine grandchildren spread across the country. Oscar and Mid were grateful in some ways. These young people were geographically distant, so the grandparents were spared knowledge of many crises until after the fact. Worries might surface, though, at the Christmas gathering in St. Louis.

First of all, there was logistics: Curtis and his family would drive 800 miles from Virginia; Carol and her crew were flying to Chicago (a business stop for Mark), then driving down; and one of Louis' children (Ethel) was coming from her study of marine mammals in Florida, another (Ben) from his banking job in Boston. At least half of the family would be dealing with some major problem, and the other half would try to find ways to help.

Louis did have space for the entire menagerie. A successful lawyer, he'd purchased what many would consider an estate: five bedroom house on a three-acre lot with carriage house converted to three-bedroom cottage and a garage-become-workout-facility with showers, bathrooms, and two rooms (billiard/table tennis and studio) that could be used to sleep at least half a dozen guests. What he didn't anticipate was the challenge of containing opposing viewpoints. He thought he would have an appreciative audience for his celebration of family. He ended up with an argument that threatened to continue into the next century.

The line between humorous disagreement and genuine division was often hard to spot. But one phone call from Suzanne, Louis' wife, soon after Thanksgiving highlighted the kind of differences Mid—increasingly seen as the clan's matriarch—might have to mediate.

"It's Anne son Justin," she began. "We're thrilled he's coming, of course, but he wants his…'girlfriend' to come, too. They've only been dating a few weeks, and she's all of eighteen years of age. He says it's the real thing, but this stretches my definition of 'family.'"

"If Curtis and Anne say it's all right, you might as well go along. You could move another bed into the cottage. It will be a test of fire for this young woman, as that will be the scene of lively teenage sleepovers."

There were four girl cousins between the ages of 13 and 15 who knew each other well. And they loved late night gossip, board games, and pillow fights.

Suzanne sighed. "You know, I always thought it would be the California branch of the family that would break the rules. Free spirits, drop-outs, skateboarders, girls with blue hair."

"Now, Suzanne, most of that is just the rebellious nature of youth. They grow out of it. Even hippies join the chamber of commerce when they reach a certain age."

"Still, we're shocked that it's the Virginia cousins who want to write their own rules. I mean, the South, after all, with its respect for tradition!"

"You do have to admit that some of their traditions were…um, confining."

Suzanne reflected. "Okay, yes, I know. Still, it's just that Louis and I, we never went through that phase. He was such a serious student, and I had been a second mother to all my siblings before having children myself. We had to be responsible adults. But Justin says this girlfriend, Abigail, has to stay with him…in the same room."

Mid thought for a minute. "Let me have a talk with Curtis. Maybe there's a way I can appeal to his willingness to compromise."

"Sometimes, Mother," concluded Suzanne, "with the way things are going in this country I think my head is just going to explode!"

Mid would remember this statement, as more than Suzanne's mind was stretched over this holiday.

Chapter Two: Posing

As they began to fashion their stories, Oscar and Mid also tried to envision a comfortable arrangement of family members at Louis' house. They had not spent many nights there themselves, preferring to drive the two hours up and back on visits so they…well, so Oscar…could sleep in his own bed. Their chief goal now was to give him a place to retreat from commotion and Mid somewhere that the women could seek her counsel.

They assumed Louis and Suzanne's four children (and the one spouse) would occupy their own rooms, although Lucy, the youngest, might opt to stay with her girl cousins. Aunt Carol and her twin girls (thirteen in September) would probably have the cottage, along with Anne and her daughter Mary Anne. The men, Mark and Curtis (with his sons, Justin and Carl), would be fine in the garage-become-residential-gymnasium. Of course, if Justin's girlfriend—and others—showed up, shifting might be necessary.

Oscar saw it humorously as a high school science project. At dinner a week before everyone would converge on the Lindbloom house in Ladue (a wealthy St. Louis suburb), he declared to Mid, "What we have here is a number of bodies with age and gender attributes that have to be placed in a grid with the appropriate number of correctly sized facilities. There are also persons of certain authority that must be found along X, Y, and Z axes central to small groups of unpredictable agents."

"I suppose these 'bodies' have no feelings, memories, or expectations that might affect their momentum, inertia, or trajectories?"

He ignored her. "All identified objects get on trains or planes or cars leaving stations at different times, traveling at adjusted speeds, to cover a variety of distances. So, my fellow agent, when should we be loaded into the Audi and moving in order to arrive at the same place at the identical moment?"

Mid sighed. She saw the situation less abstractly and as an analogy to current world events. "It's more like a dozen of the world's most powerful nations getting ready to converge on Baghdad," she said. "They've given Saddam Hussein a January 15 deadline, as you know, to get out of Kuwait, and my prediction is we're going to be back at war. Oscar, remember we still have a daughter with significant military expertise who could be called back to active duty."

Carol had been one of the women who, beginning in 1973 (the year the draft ended) moved into increasingly vital military roles. Without enough men to handle the complex technology of weapons, guidance systems, and intelligence operations, the Army had to expand the pool of potential specialists. Carol retired three years ago to avoid further overseas deployment; she wanted to be home more with her family. Her husband Mark ran his own, increasing successful, mobile phone business and had to be on the road a lot.

Oscar dismissed Mid's concern. "Oh, they'll work out a deal in the Middle East. They always do, and Carol can insist her daughters need her at home."

Mid raised her eyebrows. "You do understand that 1) women's roles have changed in the last twenty years, and 2) that the Palestine Intifada has been raging for the last three years."

Again his thoughts went forward as if he didn't hear her. "Marianna and Christie are doing well in cross country. That means Carol has to taxi them to every practice and meet. Even though she only works part-time, there are no empty spaces in her day."

He refused to acknowledge that the girls' father had done as much—or perhaps more—child raising than Carol. But now Carol's flexible schedule freed him up to explore possible expansion of the business.

"The Middle East is a tinder box. If we go into Iraq, where will the conflict spread?"

"Not our concern." He rose from the table, getting ready for his customary leisurely evening that would begin with "Jeopardy."

Mid knew better than to push Oscar, who in recent years had become as isolationist as he was antisocial. He felt his family had done enough by sending a son and a daughter to war. Of course, he had nothing to do with "sending" them, as Carol volunteered twice against his advice and Curtis was drafted. Oscar himself had only gone to work for the Navy during WWII when it became clear that, even with his weak eyesight, he would be called up.

Still, she was unwilling to let him escape responsibility completely. "Since a happy family holiday is your concern, I'll refer all disputes to you. I think, for instance, Suzanne needs to talk to you about whether a girlfriend can sleep in the same room with one of your grandsons."

Following the "Jeopardy" formula, Oscar pretended she had given the answer for which he was supposed to provide the question. "What is a matriarch?" She growled and stepped into the utility room, official office and workplace of A Woman's Hand.

16

Oscar did worry about the role he would play at this family gathering and in the future. Perhaps because he was a professor, he'd always been seen as aloof by those meeting him for the first time or those who didn't know him well. His Scandinavian ancestry may also have contributed to the way he was perceived, as his own father, Carl, fit the stereotype of taciturn but competent, even at times arrogant about his abilities.

Oscar had valued this quality that kept people he didn't want to associate with at a distance. But now he was beginning to see that it was also a liability, especially as he aged. This realization had been reinforced recently by Curtis in a phone conversation.

On a shopping expedition to Jefferson City two years ago, Mid had fallen and badly bruised one hip, necessitating a three-day hospital stay. As a result Curtis had taken to calling them every Sunday night to make sure they were okay. He would catch them up on his family's activities, but everyone understood he was also assessing his parents' condition. Louis tended to come down at least once a month, and Carol, who sought only essential information, asked for regular reports from her brothers.

A few weeks ago, Curtis asked in his regular Sunday call, "You know those antique portraits of Grandpa and Grandma you had put in new frames?"

They had been taken in the 1920s, a prosperous time for the immigrant builder. Carl and Sadie were elegantly dressed, her natural beauty and his stoic demeanor evident.

"Yes. Your mother sent you a picture, I think. They're still in the same place in our living room. There's one of me, too, in my den. Did she send a picture of that?"

"That's what I was going to tell you about. Carl came in from soccer practice and, like a good fifteen-year-old son, leaned over his mother to give her a kiss on the cheek…and to see if she would make him a peanut butter and banana sandwich. So, he saw that photograph of you she had just taken out of the envelope. You were…what? Five years of age?"

"Four." Oscar chuckled. "I was precocious, as you know."

"Of course. Well, Anne didn't know if Carl would remember having seen them or know who they were. But he immediately pointed his finger and said, 'That's Grandpa.'"

"Good for him. I look much the same, of course, today."

"In one way you do. When she asked him how he knew that was you, he simply pointed to your hands."

"How were they the clue?"

"You're holding them in that contemplative way you do, with the fingers spread slightly, the tips of one hand touching those of the other. Sometimes you tap them together as you talk. I've seen you do it all my life, so I never thought about what it says."

Oscar was puzzled. "It means something?"

"Well, it says, 'Don't bother me, I'm thinking."

There was a pause; then Curtis added, "And it says: 'What I'm thinking is so profound you have no chance of understanding it, though, perhaps if you're lucky, I'll find a way later to simplify it to the point you might be able to grasp a portion of it.'"

"Hey, that's not what I do! It's an unconscious gesture, anyway."

"I agree. Still, I never realized it might be a bit intimidating to grandchildren. I'm so used to it, it doesn't signify anything to me. But young people sense that you're a bit more meditative or…or distant than the rest of us."

"Carol's children, the other cousins?"

"Well, I haven't done a poll, but I think it's likely." Then Curtis had concluded. "Hey, Dad, it's a good thing, They need a model of composure in this family!"

Watching "Jeopardy," Oscar realized that, after he set aside his pipe, he had put his hands in the very position Curtis identified. When Mid passed through and asked if he wanted more coffee, he grumped, "We should develop our escape plan from occupied St. Louis."

Chapter Three: Circles

In her workroom Mid studied the wooden case of her Black Forest cuckoo clock. She'd removed the works and was preparing to clean the surface. Doing more than refresh cases reduced their value to collectors. But she sold almost all her clocks locally to people who wanted a working mechanical timepiece for their home, not those who wished to decorate with antiques.

Over the years she'd developed a successful, if not particularly lucrative, business. She never charged her company for her own labor; and any year in the black was considered successful. But it pleased her to think that the list of clients whose clocks she regularly cleaned and serviced had expanded to over two dozen. And her inventory of tools, parts, and cases had increased to the point that cabinets had to be installed in her workroom.

All it had taken were a few early accomplishments, being careful not to promise too much, and word of mouth. Marian Lacy (her given and maiden names) was known throughout town as skilled in her craft and pleasant in her manner. These qualities had meant getting to know interesting people during that trying period after her children had left home.

The Rockers of Age was a parallel activity for Oscar, though it generated few continuing friendships. He met new people when he played at places like the Fairfield Country Club and the officers' club at Fort Leonard Wood; but there was seldom any follow-up. He did, though, enjoy the company of the other members of the group--Jeff, drums; Ed, bass; and Stephen, piano.

His circle of acquaintances from the university had also diminished in retirement, as he kept up with only a few of his former colleagues and increasingly avoided departmental social events. At times Mid and his children worried that his restricted social involvement would lead to behavioral changes; but he was no more or no less jovial now than he'd been when working.

The cuckoo clock case Mid was working on this evening had the intricate carving of birds and leaves in an overall design customary with cuckoo clocks. In addition to chiming on the half hour and cuckoo calls on the hour, it played a tune to which three small figures danced on a platform jutting out from the face. Studying the connected elements, Mid imagined her clock as a representation of the Lindbloom family. That analogy moved to the literal level when the phone rang and another problem for the holiday gathering was laid at her feet.

"Listen, Mom," Carol said, characteristically without any lead in, "I have to object to the men getting the gym at Louis'. My girls like regular, vigorous workouts. They need unlimited access to the equipment--the stationary bike, the treadmills, the weights. Well, and so do I."

"And how are you, my child?"

"What? Oh, fine. Can you talk to Louis? You're such a diplomat."

"And Mark, he's well also?"

"Of course. Hey, are you afraid to speak forcefully to Mr. Chief Justice? You know I can use my command voice, if necessary; but I don't want to spoil the holiday from the get-go."

Mid thought a minute. "You know, this might be a good task for your father. He's been evading responsibility lately. We need to draw him out of his shell."

"Good luck with that! So you'll take care of it?"

"Well, we're working on our FACTH stories right now. Don't want to look foolish in front of the grandchildren, you know."

Carol said good-bye and hung up. Mid was not offended; it was her daughter's manner.

Curtis liked to tease his sister about her direct conversional style, saying she'd never survive in his part of the country.

"The Southern Farewell, for instance," he explained one time, "is not the quick handshake, or, in your case, the salute. It's an extended process of speech and gesture repeated at multiple locations, which you would have to master for any extended stay with us."

Carol had only visited Curtis and his family in Virginia once, as her military career had her traveling all over the world. But that one short time had provided Curtis with the specific example of the Southern Farewell's general principle.

It started at the breakfast table after Carol's one night down from DC where she'd completed a two-day briefing at the Pentagon. The boys had left for school, and Mary Anne, only three, was mesmerized by her Aunt Carol in uniform. Anne wished her safe travel back to California, rose to clear the dishes, and then, seemingly out of nowhere, asked Carol if she'd found ordinary people more pleasant in Europe or Asia.

"That's kind of hard to say," Carol said, puzzled at so broad a question. "I don't always interact with civilian personnel." She turned toward the hall. Anne set the plates back down, wiped her hands on her apron, and came toward her. "Yes, I know, but I wonder if all cultures are as hospitable. It's certainly a Southern

22

tradition. They say there are many places where to refuse a meal is an offense to your hosts."

By now Carol was retreating toward the front door, Anne pursuing. Mary Anne trailed behind. "You have been quite welcoming to me," said Carol and gave her sister-in-law one of those sideways hugs, shoulder to shoulder rather than a full embrace.

Anne stepped with her through the door and, tucking her arm into Carol's, walked her out toward her car. "Curtis has had to learn these traditions. I guess you folks from the Midwest do things differently. Your father, now, he literally jumps out of the way when he and I have to cross paths. Does he keep the same distance, physically, with you?"

Carol glanced over her shoulder at Curtis, who was smiling from the front porch and holding Mary Anne's hand. He raised his free hand palm up, suggesting there was nothing he could do. Anne was engaged in the Southern Farewell, which can only be concluded by the separation of the parties involved to a distance where communication is no longer possible.

"Neither Curtis nor his brother are touchy-feely, to be sure; but you know that's the way I like it." She slid out of Anne's embrace, swung her small duffle bag across to the front passenger seat. "Okay, see you at Christmas."

Anne put one hand on the roof and one on the open door and leaned down beside her sister-in-law in the driver's seat. "But in other cultures, where they don't have as much, and maybe two or three generations live in the same small house, I would think there would be a comfortable closeness. I wonder if in America we're cutting ourselves off from each other, choosing isolation simply because we have the space to be alone."

Carol looked hard at her, then gently pulled the door closed. She lowered the window to say, "I deploy to Saudi Arabia in a month. I'll check it out there and let you know."

Anne thanked her profusely, stepping forward as the car edged away from the curve, almost as if she intended to trot beside the car at least until it reached a highway. Carol increased the speed and didn't look back.

"I wonder if it's the Army or California or your Lindbloom genes that make her standoffish," she told Curtis as she walked up to the porch. "I love your sister, very much, of course. But Suzanne and I are able to communicate so much more easily."

Taking a toothbrush to the birds carved on the site of the cuckoo clock, Mid tried to imagine how close to this girlfriend Justin would be in public if they were indeed together at the family gathering. Even Louis' married children would probably be less likely to put an arm around a waist, plant a kiss on the cheek, dance with wandering hand than would the free-spirited Justin.

She pushed the bristles into the groves to remove dirt and grime. Everything on this clock was the color of the natural wood except for the little figures that danced as the cuckoo bird made his call, so at least she didn't have to worry about removing paint.

She thought about the cousins. Louis' younger children, Lucy and Samuel, attended a prep school where they wore uniforms, attended mandatory chapel, and studied etiquette. Justin, Carl, and Mary Anne went to small-town public schools, skateboarded in punk outfits, played in ad hoc rock bands. They had gotten along most of their young lives, but, as Mid knew from her siblings-- and her children--adolescence exaggerates youth's worst tendencies.

If the weather was mild in St. Louis this winter, they might burn off energy in friendly basketball games on Louis' outdoor court. And snow could lead to physical exhaustion from sledding, building snowmen, friendly snowball fights. But any combination of unpleasant weather and restricted activity might promote antagonisms.

Mid looked at the red, white, and green figures on the clock set out her worktable. Little elf-like creatures in lederhosen and caps were pulled in a circle; their feet rose and fell as they danced. Then she imagined them turning on each other and banging their fellows over the head with the black numbers they'd ripped off the face of the clock, then asking Mid to put everything back together again.

Chapter Four: Windows

Mid didn't want to admit that the twin who was four minutes younger, Marian, was her favorite grandchild any more than Oscar would confirm that he had a special liking for Louis' boy, Samuel. Of course, they loved them all. But Sam was planning on getting a Ph.D. in mathematics, and Marian had declared at age ten that she would become a doctor and help poor people in far-off lands. Sometimes it's nice when things skip a generation.

Oscar had often worried that Louis' seriousness and Suzanne's Catholic training would make their children too conformist. But Sam had been cleverly rebellious. He managed to reject his parents' opinions without offending them. He could be in church without being of the church, as his apparently idle thoughts about stained class windows revealed. Delivering these ideas to a sympathetic grandfather in a public setting also made it hard to criticize him.

"Your father, my grandfather, was Lutheran, wasn't he, Grandpa?" Sam had asked while the six St. Louis Lindblooms were in Fairfield to celebrate Oscar's birthday once. "I mean so many Scandinavians are, or least were, until the most recent generations." He had always been precocious, so this observation at age twelve didn't surprise the group.

"He was raised in that church, but didn't go very often in this country unless he was visiting with his family in Assyria." Oscar was leaning back in his recliner and smoking his pipe after the celebratory dinner and cake. "Why do you ask?"

26

"Well, I went with a neighborhood friend to one of the area Lutheran youth group meetings, and I was pleased at the openness and brightness of the church building."

"That's different from your church?" Oscar, who, professing to be a practicing agnostic, had never attended mass with his son's family...or, for that matter, been in any church since he'd started college. Whether he was father of the groom or the bride, he felt it was a concession to appear at the weddings of his children.

"You see," Sam went on, "all the wood in our church is dark--the pews, the floors, the altar. While there are colors--the vestments, the robes, and so forth--there's very little light in the sanctuary. It's the stained glass windows, I guess, that make everything dim, somber, crowded."

"The windows don't add color?"

"They do; but, then, that's not their purpose. As I understand the Roman Catholic tradition, church windows are there to shield us from the outside world, not provide access to it."

Suzanne was concerned. "You're not saying the windows are barriers, are you, imprisoning the people?"

"No, not that. The goal is to shape our perception of the world outside through religious icons. The forms in the windows--the shepherd and the lamb, the holy mother, the children of God—help us to find those things outside the church. The windows are a kind of outline of what matters, the framework within which our experience should be shaped."

Suzanne was pleased, though Oscar and Louis suspected a double meaning in the boy's logic. "My son is a natural Jesuit theologian," claimed Louis. "I wish he would take this up with Father William, but he says he doesn't want to bother a busy man."

Sam continued, "Did you know that incense, which is now thought to be a helpful accessory to worship--like music or the poetry of prayer--was originally used to cover up the smells of the commoners? The lords and ladies of the manor had sensitive noses."

"So?" asked his mother.

"I'm just saying we need to be aware that the regular elements of our worship often had a very practical origin. There's some value in opening up practices to light and fresh air." He gave a sly grin. "Not that I'm unhappy in our church, Mother. Not at all."

Sam's pleasant acceptance of their conventions pleased his parents, but his ability to stretch the definitions of orthodoxy amused Oscar. He felt a kindred spirit in this grandson, believing that he was free-thinking as he'd been when that age. Mid, however, worried that, at sixteen, he might unsettle the peaceful acceptance of differences within the larger family.

She could imagine the behavior of Sam's cousin Justin and the girlfriend Abigail having a ripple effect spurred by the teenager's seemingly innocent questions. Mid felt the younger cousins were, for different reasons, somewhat naive. She hoped she could help soften for Marian, her favorite, the drama that comes when a girl finds herself in a woman's body.

Marian had been intrigued by her grandmother's brief service in the Red Cross during World War II. Carol couldn't provide her daughters with detail about her own Army career because so much of what she did was classified. But she had always been proud of her mother for driving a Red Cross Clubmobile, a truck that delivered donuts to the troops in WWII.

Carol explained to her girls that that period in history allowed women to step outside of the usual boundaries, and her grandmother's overseas experience stuck Marian as a romantic adventure. When Oscar and Mid spent a week with the family in California, Marian demanded to know all about her donut days. It was the longest time the twins had spent with their maternal grandparents since their birth.

"Momma told me you were knitting for soldiers during the war before you went off to make donuts for them. Can you teach me to knit? When I'm a doctor, I'll also have to stitch up patients who have been injured."

"We can certainly start learning how to knit and even how to make donuts, but binding up wounds will have to wait. My medical training--which was a long time ago-- prepared me to conduct tests in a laboratory. Rather than stitch up patients, I looked at blood cells for clues about patients' health. But, here, I have needles and yarn in my bag."

Some years after graduating from Archer College in Baltimore, Mid had gone back to school to certify as a medical technologist. Her profession and a desire to travel eventually took her from New Jersey to Missouri, where she met Oscar. Both were working at the state health department. Many years later, after her children had left home, she began to volunteer at the hospital lab in Fairfield, though it was usually only a few hours a day. She pricked fingers and made slides.

"What's fun," she told Marian, "is to think how women who lived centuries ago were making the same scarfs or sweaters for their family that we knit today. For instance, this sweater I'm working on for your cousin Ethel--a marine biologist--is like the ones fishermen have worn for generations. I'm going to have a row of fish swimming around the chest."

Mid had been taught to knit by her own grandmother, and the practice had always relaxed her and given her a sense of accomplishment. She regularly perused magazines for new patterns and stopped by yarn shops to find unusual material. She felt a membership in the worldwide coterie of women who share knitting history and technique.

"Momma bought me some needles already, after we knew you were coming. She got out a scarf you knitted for her when she was going to be in Sweden for a month. It has mountains with snow on the top."

"I remember that. I wanted to picture the land where she would be. It was a challenge to follow the pattern, which came from Grandpa's Cousin Ilsa."

"Did you know that Madame Lafarge secretly wrote the names of her enemies in her knitting? Uncle Curtis can tell you about it. He knows everything about Dickens and *A Tale of Two Cities*."

Mid laughed. "I've read that myself. Fortunately, we have no enemies to go after."

Now that an older Marian would be in a mix of cousins over Christmas, Mid hoped she would find none whose names should be worked into a scarf of retribution. She also hoped the one name written in her own private list of difficult people would stay hidden in her heart.

Her granddaughter-in-law Elizabeth (wife of Louis' oldest son Benjamin) had a tendency to criticize Suzanne for how she decorated or what she cooked or the way the grounds were landscaped. And Mid had not always kept her tongue in those situations, despite her granddaughter-in-law's frequent references to her own refined education at East Coast finishing schools. Daughter of an Army brigadier general, she had a habit of assuming authority.

Christmas would be a golden opportunity for Elizabeth to snipe; and Mid was determined to defend her daughter-in-law, even if it meant becoming a new target for criticism. She trusted--wrongly, it turned out--that Oscar would be oblivious to any discussion of propriety. His sudden, uncharacteristic attention to the social milieu around him helped bring one more source of family tension to the surface.

Chapter Five: Insignia

"Want to hear a draft of my Far Away Close to Home story?" Oscar asked Mid two days before they were to start for St. Louis. He had wandered into A Woman's Hand and was watching her oil the works of her cuckoo clock. "You can give me some tips and warnings."

"Sure, but you'll have to do the same for me in another day or so."

"Deal. But maybe I should wait." He waved several sheets of typewriter paper at her. "'High Points' might set the bar too high for you. You know, some of the children thought I should be handicapped as a storyteller."

Mid chuckled and spun one of the gears of the clock mechanism. "Let's say rather that you'll inspire me to make the most of my limited ability."

"Fair enough. So my tale begins with a sensitive young man growing up in an average city of a plain state during a regular time. But this youth is not at all ordinary."

"I assume this is a version of you."

"He could be someone I knew growing up. Anyway, he—let's call him Oswald, for now—Oswald feels hemmed in by convention and by the restrictions of limited resources. His father works hard as a builder; and his mother, a former farm girl, at times has had to take in laundry. But he wants to attend a great university, distinguish himself as a world-class architect—as well as a talented jazz musician—one day returning to his home town a hero."

"He'll settle down, marry his high school sweetheart, become mayor, run for Congress, eventually become President?"

"Of course not. His empire will be of the mind, not the state. He wants to build skyscrapers that give visitors a sense of freedom from worldly restraint. They won't understand why they feel uplifted, but he will know his vision has inspired thousands of men and women."

"Now I see this can't be you. You love boundaries and limits and routine. The automobile seat belt could be on your coat of arms."

"Ha! True geniuses must restrict themselves in order to free others. Anyway, Oswald will be recognized as the designer of these magnificent structures and a fine musician, but his true pleasure will come from those who enter into his buildings of steel and of melody."

"Speaking of buildings, did you get your favorite oatmeal cookies at Aldi's today? You know the jar is nearly empty."

"Huh? Oh, yeah, in the cupboard…I think. Anyway, one clear, winter night, despondent about his prospects, this enlightened youth decides to scale the town's water tower."

"If he's going to jump, I don't want to hear this story."

"No jumping, just a bold act to set himself apart from the herd. He carries cans of paint."

"He's going to write 'Osward loves Beatrice' in bright gold letters, right?"

"If he did, it would be in Latin. But his scheme is more about himself than his beloved."

Mid gazed out the patio doors. "Do you remember that water tower we saw in…where was it? Arkansas? It was in a town famous for growing peaches. They had painted the water tower to look like a giant peach."

Oscar laughed. "I do remember, because the tower didn't look so much like a peach as a baby's bottom. The place where the stem was is…um, you know; and there's a kind of crease up one side that creates two…well, cheeks."

"I think you claimed at the time it was the comely farmer's daughter's behind, but I hope Oswald escapes misinterpretation of his art."

"Oh, he knew what he was doing. He drew a recognizable cultural stereotype of the day, a new comic book character."

"Let's see: when would this be? Late 1930s—Mickey Mouse?"

"Of course not. He painted a bright red Superman in flight up from his home town—one fist raised, the cape fluttering, his gaze piercing the sky."

"Did Oswald get the credit for his work? He didn't inscribe his painting, did he?"

"His signature was clever enough that his friends recognized him as the artist, but town officials could not identify who defaced public property. You see, the 'S' on Superman's costume is sort of made up of an 'O' on top and…um, another letter beneath it. So, it appeared to most viewers that he didn't get the drawing right, but he was actually inserting his initials into the design."

"Ah, I see—Oswald…uh, Lobotomy."

"Oswald, correct; lobotomy, no. In fact, he did even better than he'd anticipated, as the 'S' was also the first initial of the town's name; so many people thought it had been drawn by the city—if poorly—to advertise its growing importance in the state."

"Let's see. There's an Air Force base in your home town, or at least there used to be."

"Smokey Hill Air Force Base came to Salinas a bit later, after the war started. But it did fulfill the city's aspirations. The B-29 Superfortress flew out of there, and later my fair city was a center for the Strategic Air Command. But our boy genius didn't see this coming. He was sure America would never go to war."

"That reminds me: this is supposed to be a story 'far from home.' Did the artist go off to war, then?"

"No, but he did travel. Many years later Oswald went to Long Island. He'd become a research scientist and was asked to contribute to a very important project at Brookhaven National Laboratory, where, of course, he was 'far from home.'"

Mid was running the weight chains that power the cuckoo clock in and out of a cleansing solution. Wearing rubber gloves, she fed the links into a trough, brushed them with a toothbrush, and them pulled them out the other end to dry on an old bath towel.

"That's interesting. My husband spent a sabbatical there in the mid-1960s. I thought he was just goofing off, but some kind of publication about fluids came out the next year."

"'Some sort of publication'! I redefined the nature of liquid matter, but you wouldn't understand. Now Oswald, he had an epiphany."

"Hmm, that reminds me of climbing the Montauk lighthouse out on Long Island."

"Right. We found out we had gotten too sedentary in our later years. We huffed and puffed and barely got to the top."

Oscar smiled but remembered something else: how the view of the ocean had not been inspiring, but the opposite. Having grown up on the plains, he had always loved open spaces, grand views. He thrilled at the fields of Kansas wheat rippling with the wind, neighborhoods of the city seen from a rooftop fading into the prairie, a thin ribbon of river trailing off into the horizon. But that view of the Atlantic unsettled him in what he called "the youth of old age."

"Sure. But Oswald is young and healthy. He scaled the ladders and platforms easily."

Oscar and Mid had been at Montauk on a rare, still day, the sea calm, blue sky above with no clouds to provide perspective. If he hadn't put his hand in hers, a primal fear of falling might have overcome him. He claimed his breathlessness came from the 137 steps he had climbed.

"Did our young man have his epiphany there," Mid asked, "his eyes opened by the lighthouse beam to reveal that he was, in fact, Superman?"

"Better. At the top of that lighthouse Oswald saw scratched on the inside frame of a window a tiny, unobtrusive Superman 'S.'"

"Ah, another teenager, another generation, had defaced public property."

"Probably, but it made Oswald realize something. Superman had X-ray vision and telescopic vision, but it was never clear that he was exceptionally smart. Just strong, fast, invulnerable to everything but kryptonite. Oswald, on the other hand, had the ability to understand what happened inside of matter. He didn't see beneath the clothes of the comely farmer's daughter or what happening on the other side of a brick wall, but he could write the formula that described the forces that control substances, what governs the natural world."

Mid looked up at him, pulled off her gloves, and rose from her stool. "Not more powerful than a single locomotive, then, but able to unlock the secrets of the universe for the minds of fellow scholars and generations of students."

She gave him a kiss on the cheek and a pat on his behind. "Nice story, Clark Kent." To herself she thought: nut not a story the grandchildren will understand. And it's exactly the kind of braggadocios claim that can irritate his sons and his son-in-law.

It never occurred to her that it would be something she herself unintentionally let slip that caused the most concern at the family gathering.

Part II: Mid

Chapter Six: Quarters

Mid children's generation claimed they related to each other as cooperative fellow citizens, avoiding their fathers' tendency to see others as competitive rivals. Baby-boomers were angels of tolerance, proponents of equality, disciples of opportunity.

Women of the same age insisted, too, that sisterhood bound them together despite differences of class, ethnicity, education. The term "cat-fight" was offensive to them, and if they felt resentment rise in their deepest being, it was surely caused by, and should be directed at, men. But Mid had observed antagonism still emerged when core feelings clashed.

Often the issues people fought about were proxy ones, superficial matters that stood for deeper concerns. She recalled her sons and husband battling at Ping-Pong in the house on Limestone Drive, unaware of forces within them that affected the outcome.

The basement room was so small that there was less than three feet between each end of the table and a wall. The Lindblooms could not back up the way tournament players did in returning hard slams. And a close ball hit at a sharp angle could lead to an opponent's paddle bumping into a wall on one side or the other. But it was the players' pent up emotions that more often determined winners and losers.

Mid recalled one winter contest some years ago. The boys began posting scores on a chalkboard, determined to claim a weekend championship. Oscar had drawn up a certificate and promised a princely award of twenty-five cents to the winner. Worried about his own father in Jefferson City, though, he said he would only be an observer himself. Carl had been suffering heart trouble all fall; and Oscar had driven up to Jefferson City earlier that week. Sadie insisted he was doing better every day.

The best-of-seven-game showdown was dramatic, as both boys had become skilled in competition with opponents at their schools. Balls hit hard at times ricocheted off the walls and flew back across the net. Slammed into a corner, another might sometimes shoot up to hit the overhead light or rebound into the little window casement under the ceiling. Now and then one player was stung by a ball striking a knuckle or an ear or a forehead. The cracks of contact and the grunts of effort echoed from hard surfaces in the tiny space.

"Deuce," declared Curtis grimly in the rubber game. He'd come from behind to tie and felt momentum was on his side.

"Clearly your opportunity, little brother," smiled Louis. He was using the psychology that had worked for him when they were both younger and his brother was half a foot shorter.

Curtis retaliated by mocking his brother's practical mindset and regimented lifestyle. "Your opportunity to prepare an argument for why fewer points means victory in legalese?"

Mid had been saddened by the anger and frustration that grew out of such determined contests. Working in the kitchen at the top of the basement stairs, she could hear screams, the occasional flinging of a paddle, male teenagers' language.

"Can't you make those boys behave a little better down there?" she would beg Oscar.

"It's a coming-of-age ritual. If it wasn't happening here, it would be out on the streets. At least we know what's going on with them."

Both sons had matured during their high school years; but they also knew the other's sore spots, and gamesmanship was considered part of fair play.

After another furious rally, Curtis claimed the advantage a second time. Oscar came down the stairs and sat on a middle step to watch quietly.

Louis' deliberate consistency led to another deuce, then to his ad, then to another deuce. "I don't want you to be distracted, Curt, but I think Dad took a phone call for you earlier." He winked at his father. "Some girl who's…interested." Curtis had had a number of girlfriends, as opposed to Louis, whose focus on his studies made it seem he might have chosen celibacy.

"I think the call was from a fellow student of yours who wants to borrow your slide rule, but I told her it had gone limp." Curtis had a capacity for coarseness that irritated Louis.

Though concentrating intensely on the game, both boys glanced now and then at Oscar. He always liked to kibitz as they played, but tonight he was silent, smoking his pipe and not really watching the game.

When Louis finally prevailed and asked for the winner's certificate and his quarter, Oscar seemed to come back from some place far away. "Boys," he said, "I'm sorry to tell you this, but your grandfather passed away. I got the call from Grandma a little while ago."

Oscar had been in awe of his father all his life and passed this veneration on to his sons. All three knew of Grandpa's hard childhood in Sweden, starting over with nothing in a new country, staying one step ahead of bankruptcy through the Depression. That he would deteriorate so quickly, physically and mentally, over a few months had been difficult for them. Their Thanksgiving holiday had been muted by seeing Grandpa barely able to rise and greet them, by Grandma's tired insistence that he was getting better, and by her refusal to accept any help.

On the night of the epic table tennis contest, none of the men seemed to know what to say or do. They would go up to Jefferson City the next day and again later for the funeral. The following summer they helped Grandma move to a small apartment in Fairfield. But table tennis in the basement felt uncomfortable, and they were relieved when their parents moved across town and the table was set up on the outside covered patio.

When Mid first saw Louis' home gym, she was pleased at the tall ceiling, the more than adequate space, the track lighting perfectly positioned. Here was an appropriate venue for table tennis, she thought. No one bumping against walls or deliberately trying to smack a ball into an opponent's sensitive body parts. Angry words would have room to dissipate, and the smells of exertion would thin as they traveled.

The facility would be especially nice this Christmas if the girls were competing with boys. Less chance of stray physical contact, enough space for decorum, furnishings that called for polite language. However, even in civil discourse, Mid knew, cracks could appear in the social fabric. One had existed for many years in the family.

From the moment she got to know her fiancé's family, Anne had found it difficult to understand Carol's military past. She herself was close to being a pacifist. Living in an academic environment, she automatically assumed those close to her shared her belief in

42

peacemaking over the use of force. This summer her political views about the ultimatum given to Iraq had led to an uncomfortable exchange with her sister-in-law.

Anne and Curtis were in Fairfield for a short visit before heading further west to visit old friends. Mid had Anne pick up the extension so she could wish her nieces in California a happy birthday; but before she got on, the conversation strayed to a discussion of the annexation of Kuwait and the naval blockade of Iraq. Carol was telling her mother it wouldn't work.

"But the blockade is working," interrupted Anne. "Economic sanctions and diplomatic efforts will defuse the crisis and bring Saddam Hussein to the bargaining table."

Carol explained, "There's so much involved in the area that we don't know about--past rivalries, post-colonial transformations, tribal hostilities. The battle for power in the region wages across and within borders; and outside forces are supplying weapons and know-how."

"I worry about what our own generals will do. Their careers demand combat, you know, and often drive us to war."

"Excuse me?" said Carol frostily.

"Well," Anne insisted, not thinking about her audience, "there are also a lot of companies that stand to profit from military adventures."

Carol took a deep breath. "Saddam Hussein has got enough customers for his oil to keep the country going indefinitely. And he has everything to gain politically by defying the United Nations, which his people see as a pro-Western institution. He fought a costly desert war with the Iranians for ten years, inflicting untold damage on his own citizens."

Anne almost realized she had gone too far. "Well, I do hope you're wrong. We don't need one more overseas conflict. Your brother certainly wouldn't want to see another generation of young people sent off to fight in a lost cause." Carol hung up, and Mid knew both parties to this conversation would stew about the other's views for weeks or more.

This may have been when Mid came to feel close quarters were sometimes a good thing for altercation. Having to work out their antagonisms in the small area of a basement room had been good for her boys. Anne and Carol might have to share space for an extended period to iron out their differences; but she wasn't sure she wanted that to happen this Christmas.

Chapter Seven: Harmonies

Mid never could understand how her right-leaning daughter and her left-leaning daughter-in-law shared the same religious affiliation: both were Episcopalian. When their families were together, they enjoyed going to church as a group. But their shared body of belief certainly didn't extend to all political or social issues.

Curtis had explained the famous Anglican "middle way" to his mother, historically a compromise between the formal rigidity of the Roman Catholic Church and the independence of Protestantism. (Many of Mid's friends just called that being wish-washy.) And Mid knew not all members of any denomination understood their creed in exactly the same way.

"You know, Mom," her son had told her, "I've been studying British literature since I was eighteen, and both poetry and prose echo the liturgy of the Church of England. So it seems a perfect home for me, and I just don't quibble about complicated theoretical matters and how they relate exactly to social issues."

Curtis had dropped out of Sunday school when he entered high school; and since his father dismissed organized religion as intellectually crippling, Mid was unable to object. Her daughter had been less rebellious, but participated in church events as a teenager primarily for the social benefits. Later she explained to her mother that it seemed a large number of officers in the military were Episcopalians and that it had rubbed off on her.

"I think it has to do in part with the prayer book, which you can carry with you wherever you go. It gives you beautiful collects for all occasions, services for morning and evening, all the psalms. I know when I've found myself far from home, reading and studying the book make me feel connected. And not just to people back home right now, but to Christians in ages past."

Suzanne, a life-long Catholic, and Louis, a solid convert, invariably invited others in the family to attend mass with them, especially on Christmas Eve. But the West- and East-Coasters would go their own way (Mid, more or less a Baptist, alternated between the two groups); and Oscar stayed home. These different preferences would not exactly generate a diaspora in the middle of a family gathering, but it could emphasize divisions.

Taking advantage of Oscar's being out of the house one evening, Mid decided to see if she could preempt the appearance of one division by talking to Curtis. She would try to convince him to convince Justin to convince Abigail to room with the other girls. It was better that Oscar not even know about this discussion.

Anticipating their New Year's Eve gig, his group, the Rockers of Age, had planned a final practice session before they all became involved in holiday activities. They were meeting at the house of their drummer, Jefferson Davis. That really was his name, but he always shortened it to Jeff and hoped no one would make the connection. He struggled not to be perceived as reactionary; but, for over forty years a Missouri highway patrolman, he had the stern look of a man who saw no reason to adapt to a changing world.

The Rockers had lately begun to wonder if it wasn't time to change some themselves by including more contemporary tunes in their repertoire. Younger patrons were the majority at many of the places they played, including the Fort Leonard Wood Officers' Club; and they knew they were passed over for events attended by the next generation--and the one after that.

A favorite piece for older audiences was the World War II hit, "Till Then," which, as Oscar drove across town tonight, he applied to his own holiday situation: just "wait until" he had escaped occupied Ladue and was once again comfortably at home in his established routine. He thought the lyrics: "Although there are oceans we must cross / And mountains that we must climb.../ Till then, let's dream of what there will be..."

When the group was assembled, Stephen, their keyboardist, said his son had been in town recently, heard them at the country club, and made a suggestion. Stephen was a retired Methodist minister who'd lived in dozens of Missouri cities; his denomination's policy of three-year assignments for ministers kept the church flexible. "He thinks we should add a guitarist to the group. That might bring us closer to the modern age and open up some opportunities."

"Next thing you're going to say is that the guitar player should also be our vocalist," huffed Jeff. They'd always been an instrumental group, though each member did have a favorite song he might sing late in a set, late in a night. "And if it's someone as old as our grandchildren wearing drainpipe jeans and rainbow T-shirts who smashes his guitar at the end of the show, a double 'no, thanks.'

"The person I'm thinking of could do that but is a talented musician and can tone it back for you old-timers," laughed Stephen. "And I don't know about you, but I want this group to continue even into our dotage."

"Which you are already in, if you think I'm going electric," concluded Ed, caressing his stand-up bass. He was a retired professor of mechanical engineering who restored string instruments as a hobby.

Oscar hadn't ever considered the group being larger, as the four enjoyed playing together but kept their personal lives separate. A newcomer could upset a delicate chemistry that had existed for decades. But the idea that The Rockers might become so dated that no one would want them for events was unsettling. This was his social life outside of home.

He could be happy for long stretches watching his regular television shows, re-reading favorite novels (classic adventure tales like Edgar Rice Burroughs' Martian books), and reminiscing about the good old days (though unsure about exactly when they began or ended). And he felt a satisfactory, if vicarious, sense of interaction with others when Mid told him about the people she met in her clock repair business. But he would miss the practices and the performances with these "friends of long standing" (a phrase he used instead of "old friends.")

"Maybe we'd better hear Stephen out," he offered. "We want to avoid becoming an extinct species. And, after all, we already do a few Beatles tunes."

"You know, I think Max is home tonight and lives just a few blocks over. Why don't I suggest sitting in? Can't hurt, and you see what you think. No promises."

While Jeff and Ed were not enthusiastic, a call went out and appeared to have been welcome: Max would be there in fifteen minutes.

The Rockers had played "Get Your Kicks on Route 66" for many years, emphasizing the famous road that passed through Fairfield and nearby Waynesville, the town next to Fort Leonard Wood. Their audiences loved it and Stephen had introduced a long improvisational solo in

48

the middle that consistently brought applause. As he so often did when playing, Oscar let his mind drift across fields of memory.

He recalled the trip to Kansas Louis had taken him on recently. Mid had stayed home to work on clocks, happy that her son would be the one to participate in Oscar's nostalgia. Seeing the small houses he'd lived in as a child, the schools he'd attended, the college where he'd earned distinction, Oscar marveled at how far he'd traveled from his young self. The hopes his parents had for their only son had been more than realized.

Louis patiently listened to his father's stories, including an update on the Rockers of Age. Only once, on the drive back to Fairfield, did his own concerns interrupt Oscar's reminiscences. "You never really wanted to travel, did you, Dad? To leave Kansas, the States, go abroad?"

"Oh, as a boy, perhaps. But the imagination can take you around the world and outside of the world. I let others deal with lost luggage, people who don't understand English, insane drivers on narrow, cobblestone streets."

Louis nodded. "I understand, though Mom seems to like traveling. She's often talked about wanting to live in another country. But," he concluded, "that's not likely to happen, unless one of her grandchildren offers her an opportunity." Then he changed the subject.

Oscar brought himself back to "Get your Kicks." He marveled at the unspoken communication that had allowed the Rockers of Age to play a single song while each developed and contributed a distinctive part. What a splendid unspoken camaraderie united the four musicians!

He had worried that such a delicate mechanism could not take in a new personality. It might, he decided later, but the dynamic was even more complex than he had first realized.

Max, a talented musician, was also a woman. And she was black. When she played and sang "Where Do Broken Hearts go / Can they find their way home," for the first time, Oscar thought the words to his old song: "Till then, we'll call on each memory / Till then, when I will hold you again / Please wait till then." But as her rendition grew deeper and stronger, he recalled Natalie Cole, a young voice adding to her father's famous talent.

Over time he also began to ask if new members added into the Lindbloom family would enrich them all or introduce discord in a social unit that had been refined over many years.

Chapter Eight: Breaks

Pulling into his garage after that last practice session, Oscar thought of the song he'd written many years ago, "Route 66 Sweetheart." It had been an odd part of his youthful campaign to find love, though the song's inspiration was only an image in his mind constructed from pictures of movie stars and fictional heroines. Ideal beauty inspired him: "66 Sweetheart, wings of a dove, / Lift me to see, spirit of love." Marian Lacy would be that vision become material, and he knew how lucky he had been to find her.

Of course, not every moment in a marriage to a dream-become-tangible person is blissful, and stepping into The Woman's Hand he was met by an angry stare from his sweetheart.

"What?" he asked. "I'm not later than I said I'd be, am I? And I didn't have any errands to take care of that I forgot?"

She put down the clock spring winder, careful that the clamp was secure. If a tight spring is suddenly released, the sharp metal can slice flesh. "Oh, it's not you I'm mad with. It's your son. I'd like to know why he takes after you so much. Now he's pretending 'religious freedom' must be respected at our family get-together, which is completely beside the point."

"I thought whatever church people wanted to go to was fine. Any bickering about that should be well in the past, unless some of the grandchildren are raising the issue." He wondered if Sam might be becoming more open in his radical views.

"Absolutely right. Curtis is stretching the conventional usage of the term." She paused, then turned back to her clock. "But this is nothing to worry you about."

Mid was changing the subject both because Oscar would be no help and because she didn't want to upset him with the amount of long-distance calling she'd been doing. In their retirement, she had discretely loosened his long-standing rules about that expense. She knew this frugality was characteristic of their generation, but felt the solid income they enjoyed now ought to give her more freedom in some areas. "So, how are The Rockers of Age?"

"Perhaps not as aged as we have been. Stephen introduced a possible new member, guitarist and vocalist, Max…well, Maxine, but she goes by the shorter name. I'm guessing she's in her early forties. Anyhow, I need to put some of this new music away." He held up a handful of pages and headed back toward his study. He was, in fact, very worried that he might not be able to handle a new band member and new, unfamiliar tunes.

That left Mid to stew about the newest family worries on her own. She had gotten nowhere trying to convince Curtis to convince his son to convince his girlfriend to abide by Louis Lindbloom's house rules. He said his son would link such behavioral rules with out-of-date orthodoxy, arguing the family was trying to impost their religious views on others.

She'd reached Curtis at home, where he did a lot of his academic work. Her son's words were not reassuring. "I understand how you and Suzanne feel, Mom; and we'll do what we can. But we don't want to make the kids angry enough they'll go somewhere else for Christmas."

"I don't suppose you can threaten to kick them out of your house or cut off your support. So, are they there yet?"

"No, they went first to Abigail's in Charleston. I didn't ask about the sleeping arrangements there, afraid it would just add to their case that 'everyone else's' parents were progressive."

"You know that's the worst justification, even if it happens to be true."

Mid's sons had spent nearly all of their college vacations at home, working part-time jobs when they could. Carol took her leaves back in Fairfield, also, until she started overseas tours and had chances to see different parts of the world. Today's college students traveled to Florida for spring break; between semesters they went wherever there was snow; mid-May to late August, took road trips to visit roommates.

"It's a new age, I'm afraid," admitted Curtis. "Even though we're paying for most of his college, he's quick to remind us he's a legal adult." Justin had earned a music scholarship to study voice. It didn't cover all of his tuition, but it helped.

"I suppose Anne is fine with their sleeping together?"

"She reminds me we can't control them in Greenville, so what's the point? Plus she feels it's better to be on good enough terms that he'll ask us for help one day when he needs it."

Mid at times had to agree with her conservative friends who claimed standards were eroding But she later assured her daughter-in-law that "Justin and Abigail seem to understand the situation."

"That's such a relief," said Suzanne. "We don't want anyone to be upset over the holiday, especially now that Benjamin is thinking of leaving his position at the bank and enlisting in the National Guard or the Reserves. He's got me and Louis concerned."

"Enlisting! I thought he was going to win some look-alike contest and get rich."

"Oh, that's a pipe dream coming from Elizabeth. 'The General,'" (that was the way she referred to her son's father-in-law), "says funding for the military has dropped so low we're not ready for the next war, which will begin, he claims, in just a matter of months."

Like many in her generation Mid had embraced the idea of a "peace dividend" after the fall of the Berlin Wall. Military spending was to be reduced in favor of domestic programs, a number of which, like Social Security, were important to retired people. Of course, other voices were raised in opposition to cutbacks for the armed forces. And the threat posed by Saddam Hussein's' invasion of Kuwait gave new energy to their demands.

Mid asked, "But don't we still have our armies, our ships, our bombers?"

"All the branches are understaffed, according to Elizabeth. And, if we do have to fight overseas, we'll need men to protect the home front."

Mid knew it would be useless to suggest sending Peace Corps volunteers, not soldiers, to developing nations, AmeriCorps teachers rather than riot police backed by the National Guard into inner cities. If our military was stretched too thin, the way to give it more power, Mid felt, was to reduce our global commitments and strengthen social networks at home.

Mid concluded, "Surely it would be best not to discuss this in front of the whole family. As you say, we should all enjoy the holiday and each other. Who knows when the whole clan can gather again, as far flung as we are."

"Louis will do what he can, but Elizabeth--you know Elizabeth...she's capable of bringing it up while he's cutting the turkey. Oh, dear! That's another thing. Christie has become a vegetarian. She won't eat what the rest of us are having, and I don't know what to fix her."

"Deviled eggs, dear. They supply the protein. It won't be a big issue."

Mid already knew about her niece's decision not to eat meat. Apparently, she'd done a research project at her school that connected vegetarianism to movements for world peace. If we don't kill animals for food, the argument went, we're less likely to kill each other.

"Oh, thanks, Mother. That will be easy. And I'll have plenty of peanut butter available for sandwiches." Mid decided not to tell her to look for organic brand with no oils, sugars, or preservatives. "Now, there's just the Christmas skit Sammy is cooking up."

"Skit? Aren't the kids a bit old for that?"

As long as there were little ones, parents and older children had staged a nativity scene and acted out a drama connected with the birth of Jesus. They all got to devise a costume, propose story lines, occupy themselves so that the focus was not simply on presents.

"I said so, but Sam and Lucy had already written Carl and Mary Anne. They're apparently going along, and none of them will reveal the plot. It'll be a 'surprise,' is all they'll say."

Images of unlikely contemporary settings for the ancient story came to Mid's mind: an automobile garage in a decaying urban neighborhood; some abandoned saloon in a ghost town out West; a moonshiner's hut deep in the Ozark woods. Dialogue alone could offend the pious-- "Y'all need some hootch before you curl up in the hay?"

Mid thought about how one used to be able to count on polite social discourse, especially where religion was concerned. She wondered what her grandchildren from Florida to Boston to California would agree was proper.

The Catholic mass was still said in Latin in some places, but that was fading. Episcopal services were considered formal, but the service where Curtis and Anne attended was "low church." None in her family "spoke in tongues," but a boundary-stretching Christmas skit could provoke a tower of Babel in Louis' mansion.

Mid felt some rituals, like confession and absolution, bound up natural desires to a point of repression. But right now she thought more repression might not be so bad.

"The global mobile phone market? What exactly is that?" Oscar asked Carol when she called the day before he and Mid were ready to drive into St. Louis. Despite his enthusiasm for exotic cars and their features, he had not included a GMS cellular hands-free telephone in his Audi V-8. Too futuristic, he claimed, though he had no objection to the eight-speaker Bose sound system. Car radios, he reasoned, had been around for decades.

"Mark says there are emerging markets around the world, and there are good reasons to expand." Carol was calling from Chicago where her husband was attending a telecommunication conference. The weather was bad, so she and the girls were stuck in the hotel.

"That sounds like good news. I'm sorry I don't pay too much attention to his business. But if he means the two of you are even more secure financially, I'm pleased."

With her military pension, her consultant work for a security company, and Mark's business they were already more than comfortable. The Bay Area in California seemed to be exploding with the research and development of new electronic equipment and services.

"It's promising, but I suspect it may mean more travel for him overseas. After all the times I was away from home in the Army, I've come to value being in one place."

"Well, you can stay home while he jets about. It's kind of traditional for mothers, anyway, and certainly good for your daughters."

Perhaps, thought Oscar, he should have kept that thought to himself. He would also have to be careful not to repeat his sentiment to Mid. Except for Suzanne, the women in his life seemed to have made a commitment to stretching old definitions of gender roles.

"Humph," said Carol. "There may be times when we travel with him. Anyway, I was just calling to let you know the driving might be a bit slow from here tomorrow. The storm is spreading to the south and east. Pass it on to Mom so she won't worry."

In his calculations about the Lindbloom family gathering, Oscar had not factored in the weather. Figures in his mental schematic moved across a flat plain without friction: no wind or ice adding to or decreasing from their speed. There were also no extra-Lindbloomian projectiles crossing the territory, no loss of force propelling objects to their destinations, no alterations in the methods employed to complete the operation.

He knew he was being careful in such thinking to dismiss moments—occurring more frequently than he wanted to admit—when the basic patterns of the world around him seemed fuzzy. Several times at the Rockers of Age rehearsal he had lost track of the melody, the key, the timing of solos. Surely this was a reaction to a new musician, not a symptom of failing abilities.

In a larger frame of reference, though, he trusted his experience and intelligence were correctly predicting his children and grandchildren's future. There would be a steady progression of all the elements that had allowed him, after the Depression and a world war, to enjoy a productive, satisfying life—educational opportunities, economic growth, progress in industry.

Especially now that Mikhail Gorbachev was loosening the reins of Communist party control and satellite states were breaking away from the Soviet Union, America seemed poised to define the terms of world trade and industry. Our military might would not be challenged.

China was a backward state, Africa and South America remained far behind Western countries in development, Europe was still fragmented despite the fact that some countries were working to reduce tariffs and encourage mutual cooperation. American economic growth had increased Oscar and Mid's retirement nest egg more than they had anticipated, and their children, building upon this stable platform, would do even better. And yet, thought Oscar, and yet…

He recalled the satisfaction he'd felt when he and Mid had moved into their first house. Their neighbors were veterans returned from war and professionals taking jobs at the college or with light industry, both shifting into a peacetime mode. There were also doctors, lawyers, and businessmen providing services to a stable but growing community.

The solid context of that time seemed to Oscar implied in the sophisticated design and function of his Jaguar 3.4 sedan nestled in the attached one-car garage. Polished mahogany dashboard, rich leather upholstery, state-of-the-art engine. Every morning on Limestone Drive he pushed the starter button and thrilled to the hum of his six cylinders. He would crack the window to hear the throaty sound of the exhaust, back out into the driveway, cruise the one mile to his office in the physics building, pleased that no one in Fairfield owned a similar model.

Why, then, was there always an oil spot on the floor of his garage?

He took the car to the dealer in St. Louis. "It's not a fast leak," he admitted. "I check it once a week, and the oil level's not noticeably down. But it shouldn't be leaking at all."

"I've never had a problem with this model. Let us take it back to the shop."

The mechanics removed the oil pan, replaced the seals, told him it would be fine. But at the end of the week, the blot was there again. He'd put newspaper weighted down with sand to gauge the rate of the leak and to make cleanup easier. He also hung a tennis ball on a string from the garage roof; when his windshield bumped into the ball, he knew the engine was positioned in the same spot. At the end of the week he had a stain between three and six inches wide.

He wondered if the oil could possibly be from another source, like the aged motor scooter Curtis, then a high schooler, rode. He was supposed to park it beside the garage, but Mid reported he sometimes pulled inside when the Jag was gone and he would be going out again.

"Mid, keep an eye on Curtis. No working on the scooter in the garage, no parking in there even for a quick turnaround. I've got a problem to solve."

Mid promised to watch, but he wasn't convinced she was taking this seriously. Curtis was a charmer, and she had a hard time being strict with her boys.

He went to the library to research the problem. One of the first things he learned was that it might be endemic to the brand. In a trade magazine one car reviewer reported that Jaguar salesmen wore soft soled shoes that absorbed oil drops in show rooms so that customers' suspicious were not aroused. There were also stories of mechanics using heavy oil to slow leaks.

In his darker moments, Oscar suspected Mid of dropping grease on the paper. She had wanted her own car for some years, but he argued they couldn't afford it. She countered that two less expensive cars would cost little more than one luxury sedan. Perhaps she was trying to make him unhappy with the Jag so he would buy a pair of undistinguished American cars.

He made two more trips to the dealer. Each time they claimed the problem had been solved. While the oil spot's rate of spread never increased, neither did it slow. Once a week, Oscar would carry the stained stack of newsprint to the garbage and put down a new layer.

He improved his mood about the problem slightly by choosing pages from the Fairfield paper that irritated him: redundant headlines ("Opposing Parties Divided"), empty phrasing ("Mystery Deepens"), ambiguous wording ("Highway Lanes Widen Workers Claim"); contradictions ("Prospect Open at Project's Close").

Oscar was about to resign himself to the leak as a permanent condition of life when Mid proposed one more solution. "I stopped by Montgomery's the other day, just to see what used cars they had."

Oscar scowled. Montgomery was Fairfield's Ford dealer.

"And Mr. Montgomery told me about a new mechanic they've hired. He's a retired Army man who was in charge of motor pools. When he was stationed abroad he worked on all sorts of foreign makes, including Jaguars."

"And he thinks he can fix mine?"

"He guarantees it. He's seen this many times. It has something to do the car's stopping and starting, oil sloshing up on a ledge inside the block to a seal you don't suspect is involved."

Oscar decided he had nothing to lose, though he was pessimistic that some ex-enlisted man would know how to work on such a fine machine as the 3.4 engine. If it didn't succeed, Oscar would also have more evidence that women have no understanding or mechanics. And yet the problem was solved. No oil ever besmirched his garage floor again.

It took him many months to realize Mid had made a deal with Mr. Montgomery. The mechanic's unique knowledge of Jaguars was fantasy, though he was skilled. The operation was simply a charade. Former Sergeant First-Class Ramirez removed and then replaced the oil pan with no thought the leak would be found and repaired. But he announced success, and the result seemed to prove him right.

The truth was that every morning after this episode, Mid kissed her husband goodbye by the door that led out from the kitchen. When he had driven off, she stepped into the garage, removed the old newspaper, and replaced it with a new section.

Oscar eased the Audi out of the garage just after lunch, and they expected to be at Louis and Suzanne's ahead of the afternoon rush hour traffic. Interstate 44, formerly Route 66, was a smooth, four-lane ride from Fairfield to the western edge of the big city.

When Mid announced a title for her proposed FACTH story, Oscar interrupted. "Gilliane's island'? Not Gilligan's." He was thinking of the popular 1960s television sitcom in which two crewmembers and five passengers are shipwrecked on an unchartered Pacific island.

"Right. Gilliane is the great-grandmother we met when we spent five days off the coast of Maine. When was that…1980, '81? Somewhere in the early '80's."

Oscar laughed, remembering that she had decided to make up her entry in the family storytelling contest. She would show how she discovered something "close to home" while "far away"--that is, in a fictional landscape. "Ah, yes," he said. "I had forgotten for a minute."

"But now you're catching on. It was a fantastic place, not unlike the one you're thinking of, largely self-sufficient thanks to the resourcefulness of the inhabitants."

Oscar asked, "You mean no tourists descending on their rocky shores to buy local products and seduce the farmers' daughters?"

"Now and then an old geezer would wash ashore and stay to ogle the local girls. But the women already had their young men, some brought in from far flung countries."

"What? They went on shopping expeditions for blonds in Scandinavia?"

"They traveled all over the world looking for things that would thrive on the island and provide for its inhabitants, which sometimes did include brides and grooms. Over time they created a distinctive, sustainable environment, and most lived healthily into their 90's, thanks to such things as a yogurt famous for limiting the effects of aging. A granddaughter brought back a starter batch made from Yak milk by a special Russian method."

"You should have brought that formula home with us! I'm curious: why did we go there?"

"It was my dream vacation, a place I'd always wanted to visit. Finally I had the opportunity. I'd read about the island in…oh, let's say *Readers' Digest.*"

"I think you're going to learn a lot more from this fictional journey than I did returning to my Kansas childhood or taking the sabbatical at Brookhaven."

"There may have been some fiction in your account, too. Anyway, what I learned about myself far from home comes in the story's conclusion."

"Hey, you could also say you went to Cuba, the country." He pointed out the window at the exit sign for Cuba, Missouri.

"Unless we learn how to roll Havana cigars, I'll stick to my fantasy."

The new highway diverged from the old path of the Mother Road, bypassing most towns. Route 66 had once gone through the heart of every town and city; now businesses that thrived on the cross-country traffic were dying. Symbols of another era--quirky neon signs, railroad car diners, souvenir shops--were disappearing. Giant billboards now lined the highway, luring drivers to chain motels, restaurants, and tourist attractions while locally run businesses lost customers to new stores and discount places in shopping malls.

Mid went on about her imagined community, more able to preserve its past than contemporary America. "The homes on Gilliane's island were built of stone, and most were over a hundred years old. With births, deaths, and departures balancing out over the years, the population remained stable. And their way of life--fishing and farming--sustained them."

"Except that new things like Russian yogurt were brought in from time to time."

"Yes. To protect the yaks and other livestock on Gillianne's island, another of her grandchildren went to Peru and brought back llamas."

"This island is looking more and more cosmopolitan, at least in terms of its animal population. Are the inhabitants American, or are some recent immigrants?"

"The community includes people from every race, many nationalities; yet the total numbers of souls on rock and soil is less than a hundred--a microcosm of the larger world. Well, not including us. We kind of didn't count."

"That makes sense, as we were never really there."

"Still, we added to the community, as I'll remind you shortly. But let me fill in a bit more first. Gillianne's oldest son traveled to New Zealand for a special breed, Romney sheep. His brother brought back a yam from Papua New Guinea, staple for many villages there. And a cousin found special peas in Turkey and China that were highly nutritious. They learned that milk from Nepalese goats provided all sorts of necessary vitamins as well as protein."

"They weren't invaded by Alaskan wolves, or South American jaguars, or African elephants that had hidden in their cargo?"

"Ha! You're right that they had to make sure this diverse collection could coexist, with none of the species a predator. And their varied crops had to be planted in the correct rotation and location to maintain the soil's productivity. Fortunately, they're able to tap into geothermal heat, the way they do in Iceland. With greenhouses, they can harvest year-round."

"Also used to produce electricity, so you don't need to burn trees or ship in oil for power."

"And the island is small enough that people walk or bike or boat wherever they want to go. Human power drives most of their simple machines, with oxen and horses used to pull heavy loads. The town center has the general store, post office, bank, church--everything they need."

"One each?"

"Yes. We found it especially nice that there was one church that had integrated practices and ideas from all the world's religions. So ecumenical, you actually liked it."

"I went? That may be the part of your story that belies belief (so to speak). Isn't this story supposed to involve a clock somehow?"

"Yes, they had a lot of old-fashioned things--like mechanical clocks--proven products from the past. Their clock-maker had a flare up of tendinitis in his hands, so I pitched in to restore one while you figured out how to make a sailplane out of aluminum piping and canvas."

"Hmm. That's a bit vague in my memory, but I guess I could draw the blueprints, calculate stress, calibrate lift.

Younger men--or women--probably did the construction and flew the machine." Oscar thought of his love song, "Route 66 Dreamer"; the words inspired the idea of flight. "Journeying high, / You are my dream. / Above a sigh, / You are my theme."

"The Pelican was only intended for use on the island, not out over the ocean. But it was kept ready in case of emergency. Well, and as a teaching device. With few students and many well-educated citizens, the school had a flexible curriculum, delivering specialized knowledge through hands-on activities. They had a fine library free to everyone on the island."

"Tell me about the clock you fixed."

"Ah, the Seth Thomas Madonna, a thing of beauty probably worth at the time around $1,000.00. Turned out, it really just needed cleaning and adjusting. Well, there were also, I think, a few bearings that needed reboring. But none of that was where the big revelation came from. You see, I've always assumed my hobbies--knitting, clock repair, flower gardening--were about finished products—sweaters and afghans, chiming timepieces, blooming roses."

"That makes sense to me. When a set with the Rockers of Age is done, it's a finished piece of music, beginning, middle, and end just like an individual song."

"It is, but there's something else being constructed as you play or as I take a clock apart, clean and polish the pieces, reassemble everything into a whole. It's also me that gets restored or finished or put together in the process. When I showed Gilliane her working clock, I understood that I was also an improved functioning person. I had been refined yet again through my work and my association with the clock's present owner and all those who came to watch and chat."

"Ah, and that matters to you more than you thought?"

"In my advanced age, yes. And I hope I can make it matter to our family. You see, this expanded family Christmas we're driving to is not just a group photograph, a finished arrangement, everyone gathered around the dinner table. It's a process that began long before today and continues far into the future. We're a family of many individuals, evolving and surviving just as Gillianne's island community does. Even if we have some disagreements--which, unfortunately, may well happen over the weekend--the actions of each of us will contribute to the working mechanism that, for me at least, gives life meaning."

"Ah, the moral of Gilliane's Island, the soon-to-be popular television sitcom of the new year. Well, I can only hope the lesson sustains us for the next two days."

Sadly, Mid had not included two inevitable forces of change in her fantasy: health and aging. Both would take a toll at this family reunion.

Part 3: Louis

Chapter Eleven: Castle

"The dog's loose again," Suzanne informed Louis when he came into the kitchen, stamping the slush from his shoes on the mat. "I've sent Benjamin and Elizabeth to get deli meat and bread for sandwiches. Ethel's just getting up, so you need to take charge of this one."

"Understood."

Dorothy, named after escape artist Dorothy Dietrich, had a habit of slipping from her harness or out of her crate or off her run in ways no one could fathom. The miniature schnauzer was in no danger, as the estate was surrounded by an eight-feet high brick wall. But, with four acres of woods and almost five acres in open yard to roam around in, she would come back filthy and perhaps having dug in the dormant flower gardens.

"And while you're out there, check that everything is ready for the guests in the gym and the carriage house." Curtis and Mary Anne with children (and a girlfriend!) were expected by the early evening and Carol's group by midday tomorrow (assuming the weather didn't get worse). The grandparents would be the first to arrive later in the afternoon.

"Sure. That's why I came home early from the office."

He turned to open the door and then paused as Suzanne added, "When you catch her, offer forgiveness if she'll take my place in the storytelling competition. Any of Dorothy's escapades would provide better material for Far Away, Close to Home than I have."

"So, as they were able to do in the Civil War, you want to hire someone to take your place?" laughed Louis, heading out toward the garage with a pocketful of dog biscuits.

He thought his wife, an in-law, might well escape telling her story, but she'd be sure everyone else did what they were supposed to over the weekend. Having learned to be a domestic manager when she was a teenager with younger siblings, Suzanne kept this household running smoothly no matter how many friends, guests, and visitors were added to the menagerie.

Over the years, she had expanded her range so that she was consistently called on to organize charity drives, host potluck suppers, find activities for the church youth. As her children matured, she found more uses for her talents, but she still avoided addressing large groups.

What Louis worried about, though, was his own role in the future. Checking the thermostat in the carriage house, he felt once again that twinge of disappointment that had been growing since his proposal to host the family was accepted. Although everyone was coming to his house this year, and not to his parents', he felt he would not be recognized as the pater familias he had, even as boy, aspired to become. His Christmas dinner speech was designed to assert that emerging status.

Stepping from the carriage house toward the gym, he encountered his second oldest child coming from the kitchen with a coat thrown around her shoulders. Having flown in so late the night before, the only one Ethel had seen was Suzanne, who picked her up at the airport. She gave her father a hug. "Hi, Dad. I'm sure glad to be home for the holidays, but I have to tell you the weather here is quite a bit colder than where I've been!"

"But you left everything in good shape at school, right?"

"Of course. You'll get all the details from Mom. I've been sent to check the linen and then report for chores in the kitchen. But if you need help luring Dorothy back to the fold..."

"No, you go about your assigned duties. If more hands are needed in the dog hunt, Sam and Lucy will be home before too long." As usual, Louis found himself like one of the children, following Suzanne's lead rather than directing others.

As the oldest child whose youth was marked by steady application and sustained focus, Louis had anticipated a time when his parents would see him as the head not only of his immediate family, but also of siblings, nieces, nephews, and in-laws added to a larger and larger circle. This holiday gathering would imply a recognition of that status, especially if, as he'd felt recently, his father was...well, perhaps "losing a step."

The former Overton estate with its expansive grounds and multiple buildings represented an appropriate structure within which the clan could be easily organized and connected.

"Dorothy," he called, starting out on the walking/running trail. Nearly two miles long, it wound in and out of open spaces, up and down hills, across a stream, and twice by the pond. "Doro-*thy!*"

Louis felt that his bright younger brother had allowed the small college model to constrain his academic abilities; and their high-energy sister had only recently settled down after more than a decade of travel around the globe. So neither of his siblings, he believed, was in a position to be the head of the Lindblooms.

Still, current events sometimes seemed an indirect commentary on the status of their generation. As

72

diplomatic efforts were reaching a dead end in the Middle East, the nation was looking for leaders with military experience and/or militant foreign policies. And that mindset seemed to have reached out to affect Louis' professional and personal life.

Unlike his younger siblings and a number of his colleagues at his firm, he had never served in the military. Student deferments had protected him even into law school; and his luck held during the lottery years.

Immediately after the Vietnam war, having been in Army, Navy, or Air Force could be viewed negatively by employers and heads of firms who'd opposed the war. But during Ronald Reagan's presidency, and now George Bush's, attitudes were shifting. Louis began to feel he had missed a necessary requirement to be someone others turned to for advice in critical times.

He had felt no lack of self-confidence when he purchased this estate a decade ago. Already a senior partner in his prestigious law firm, Louis had reached the maturity and stature that seemed his destiny. And the history of Overton, at least its early history, provided the pattern for his own further aspirations.

In the 1920s and 1930s, the rolling hills and open pastures of this area were being sold to successful St. Louis businessmen and professionals wanting to live outside the city proper. Thomas Overton, a brewer, had purchased five acres from the Ladue family, one of the last big farmers of the region.

Hiring only the best, he walled in his compound, landscaped open areas, and put trails through his woods; he made sure the house and other buildings had all the latest features. While his two children went east for college, they returned to live at home and work in the family business, Flagg Brewery.

At the end of Prohibition the beer company was perfectly poised to expand, and Thomas bought and upgraded smaller rival breweries throughout the Midwest. He also saw the advantage of creating Flagg's own trucking company to deliver his product over new, improved highways like Route 66, as well as by rail. The Overton network grew steadily for three decades, utilizing radio and television advertising and branding its product as a symbol of America.

But the founder made several bad investments in the late 1960s. His sons and their families broke away to start a winery. Losing his wife in a boating accident, an ailing Thomas sold the neglected estate to Louis Lindbloom in an effort to avoid higher taxes and the increasing cost of upkeep. His vast empire shrank to a small apartment in a nursing home.

Seeing no sign of the wandering schnauzer, Louis made the final turn toward the house. Snow was now drifting through trees, swirling across the walkway from the gym. He saw his son Benjamin pulling away from the automatic gate at the end of his hundred-yard driveway, which passed down a lane between two rows of Bradford pears trees. He shuddered slightly, either from the cold or in anticipation of having to deal with his sometimes abrasive daughter-in-law.

"We'll need to go out again, Mr. Lindbloom," Elizabeth said as she shut the car door decisively. "My husband forgot the Gray Poupon."

"We did find this, though," said Ben cheerily, holding up a wet, muddy dog. "Dorothy was thinking of bolting through the gate, but I pounced at the pedestrian entrance." Louis took the unrepentant escapee and waved them on.

74

He and Suzanne had seen magician Dorothy Dietrich on television catch a bullet fired from a 22-caliber pistol in her teeth--a feat even Houdini had failed to accomplish. The show aired right before they brought the dog home from the breeder. Already with a reputation for sneaking away as a puppy, she was named after the magician.

Whenever he had to listen to Elizabeth, Louis felt like Dorothy Dietrich trying to stop with his mouth a bullet aimed for the middle of his head.

Chapter Twelve: Lookalikes

Suzanne helped put away the groceries Ben and Elizabeth were bringing in and listened to the latest developments in her daughter-in-law's get-rich scheme.

Looking at photographs of Ben when he was in college, Elizabeth had insisted that fall that--with some makeup, the right clothes, and a few props--he could pass for Jimi Hendrix. "See," she'd explained over the phone, "there's this look-alike contest, national, and the winner gets an all-expenses paid tip to Las Vegas and a $5,000.00 bonus."

"I don't understand," Suzanne had responded. After all, Ben was white, a fundamentally conventional young man, and a (reasonably) faithful Catholic. He played no musical instrument.

"We could use the money," Elizabeth offered. Suzanne rolled her eyes at the phone. "We need some things for our apartment--a washer and dryer, for instance. He wants to buy the latest X-box, and I've always longed to see 'Sin City.'" A psychology major at Wellesley, she projected a prosperous career for herself in personnel, or marketing, or fundraising. She shared a self-confidence with her major-general father.

Suzanne often sensed a double standard in Elizabeth's thinking. It was as if the rules she expected everyone else to live by didn't apply to her. She deserved good fortune, it seemed; others had to deal with adversity. Something else connected to this idea had stirred in Suzanne's distant memory that made her uneasy, though she couldn't pinpoint it.

"Frankly," Suzanne explained, "I've always been suspicious of windfalls. They inspire unreasonable expectations. It's like winning the lottery. The lucky ticket holders think they're destined to be favored forever, so they spend everything, go into debt, and end up alone."

"Oh, Ben probably won't win, but it's fun to fantasize. He has to work so hard, and I have my studies." And that had ended the discussion at the time.

Returning to the theme of the contest now as she folded paper grocery bags in Suzanne's kitchen, Elizabeth announced, "He's made it to the final selection, with just five other contestants! We're supposed to hear Christmas Eve. Isn't it exciting?

"Well, I hope it isn't a distraction for the family on such an important day. Why don't you two…um…watch TV or something while I get organized for dinner."

"As soon as we get the Gray Poupon, Mrs. Lindbloom. Silly boy here." she tapped Ben on the forehead with her index finger, "forgot to put it on the list." Before Suzanne could object to their going out again in the bad weather, they were throwing coats over their shoulders and pushing out into the wind and snow.

What was Suzanne remembering that triggered this alarm about look-a-likes? It was something in the past, perhaps twenty years ago or more.

She wondered if Liz had abandoned her other plan for Ben to enlist in the Army Reserves. That would be a guaranteed supplement to their income. But Suzanne didn't want to encourage him in the dangerous path his Aunt Carol had taken.

Closing the door, she saw the young couple wave to Sam and Lucy who were arriving. She gestured brother and sister toward the gymnasium, figuring that Louis could use their help with Dorothy. She would talk to Louis about their daughter-in-law's pie-in-the-sky plan later.

Sam and Lucy found Louis in the shower room, drying Dorothy with a large white towel. "Good timing," he joked. "The hard work's all done." Dorothy didn't like the bath, but the gym had a large utility sink from which she could not escape--or at least had not so far.

"We're not the ones who let him out, you know," Sam said, scooping her up and letting her lick his face. Of course, they never knew how Dorothy slipped her restraints, so no one was responsible and everyone was complicit.

"Can I move to the carriage house tonight, Dad?" asked Lucy. "I should test everything before the others arrive."

Sam added, "And I've decided--in order to polish and rehearse our skit--it would be better if I were in the gym where Justin and Carl are staying, not in my room. With the girls right next door, we can iron out all the kinks ahead of time."

There's a recipe for disaster, thought Louis: two teenage boys, one male college student, four teenage girls, and possibly a co-ed girlfriend. Out loud he said, "Your Mom and I need you both in the main house for awhile. We have to keep the grandparents happy, but when Aunt Anne arrives your mother and I will see that you're where you need to be."

"Remember we should practice with our equipment-- the keyboard, drums, guitar. This is going to be a major theatrical production."

Louis joked, "Have you drawn up posters, constructed a stage, made costumes?"

"Of course. We have the instruments, and the others are bringing their outfits. You'll be moved and changed by 'Route 66 in Palestine.'"

The workout gym did have an elevated platform, built to hold exercise equipment; and there were enough folding chairs to provide seating for the expected audience. Track lighting could be adjusted to accentuate the drama, and one of the children would have a boom box for sound. But Louis wondered whether the skit could be simple enough--and in keeping with the religious holiday--to please the whole group.

Ushering brother and sister (now holding Dorothy) back to the house, he saw Oscar's Audi pulling up to the gate. "Go inside and be ready to help Grandma and Grandpa with their things. They can park under the arch." A circular drive went under a brick porte-cochère by the side door at the end of the hall close to their bedroom. He went into the kitchen to alert Suzanne.

Putting a casserole in the oven, she asked, "Has Ben mentioned his look-alike thing?"

"He hasn't been eliminated yet?"

"No. And Elizabeth seems certain they're going to win." She began polishing the good silver, which they would use tonight and through the holiday. "When we got married, as you remember, we lived in a basement apartment and had to account for every penny we wanted to spend against what we could earn. We didn't expect money to fall from the skies."

Suzanne had met Louis in his first year of law school. With his part-time job in the library and her grocery store checkout clerk's income they joked that they were little better than poor farmers in the Depression, "Okies" fleeing down Route 66 to California.

Louis remembered how the life of a friend--actually a schoolmate of Suzanne's--had been dramatically changed by the opposite of a godsend: being number 1 in the 1969 lottery for the military draft. Jonah had counted on his student deferment keeping him out of the service--as it had for all students in good standing until Congress changed the whole system. Jonah's birthday fell on September 14, the first date drawn out of the glass jar.

Several years older, Louis got number 362. He would never have to go. But now he was having second thoughts that what had seemed good fortune then might be a burden now. Of course, Jonah's bad luck was very bad indeed.

"I guess I could try to talk to both of them about counting on chance like that, but I think I'm learning their generation simply assumes the continuing expansion of prosperity in this country, the boom years we've been in most of the time since the '60s."

"Do speak to them. I don't think our children are going to end up as well off as we are." This was an assertion she was hearing more and more at church and with other school parents. Then she smiled. "Of course, you've earned our success, sweetheart. Hard work, long hours, devotion to the firm."

If Louis occasionally felt he didn't have the respect he deserved outside the home, he never felt that way with Suzanne. She even thought her children's future would be grand simply because they were his, even though none of them looked very much like him.

Lucy was the very of image of her mother, and Ethel, though larger, shared a family likeness. But the boys were such a mix of both parents that they might be recognized as brothers but not as Louis' sons. Still, Louis had never resembled Oscar either--not as tall, with what they called big bones. His early balding made him look older,

80

whereas his father's thick black hair, parted in the middle, led people to assume Oscar was younger than he was.

As Louis thought more and more of being seen as the next patriarch, he worried about this lack of resemblance. Curtis took after Marian, so, of the three it was Carol who stood out as Oscar's child physically--well, and intellectually as well with her math skills and slender frame.

A woman could be a matriarch, of course, but Louis failed to see the youngest sibling as the chief rival for the prominence he desired. He hadn't ever considered her as the family leader before, that is; but before the holiday gathering came to an end he would see himself and his siblings in a new light.

Chapter Thirteen: Paths

Louis went to the downstairs guest room (which had its own bath) to help Sam and Lucy bring his parents' things inside. He decided he would have his discussion about serendipity with Ben and Liz after he—seasoned lawyer—had mentally prepared his case.

"No need to hurry unpacking," he explained, shaking his father's hand and giving his mother a hug.

His Virginia sister-in-law said the handshakes and hugs this family exchanged were stiff. They didn't embrace each other face-to-face as Southerners did, sometimes planting a kiss on one cheek; instead each put a hand lightly--and briefly--somewhere on the surface of the other. They were all connected by family but always insisted keeping a distinct distance from each other.

"We're fine here for a few hours, Louis," said his mother. "We still have some presents to wrap, and Louis is considering a complete rewrite of his Far Away, Close to Home tale."

"We've worked up a fine drama for our part in the celebration, Grandma," added Sam. "'Route 66 in Palestine.' You know, Dad's office sits on a historic place on the Mother Road."

Oscar answered, "Right. But remember growing up in Jefferson City and in Kansas, I'm not so caught up in the mythology of the old road. I suppose you've read *The Grapes of Wrath*?"

"That's what got him on the theme," Lucy said. "Who knew something in one of his classes would actually take root in his adolescent brain and blossom in a productive enterprise?"

82

Mid wondered, "I can understand Palestine being the setting for a story about Jesus, but I'm not sure they had paved highways at the time."

"Route 66's disappearing today," Louis reminded them. "So, maybe the Romans once built a brick or stone road as advanced as their aquifers, and it was destroyed in later times."

The last stretch of the famous highway had been decommissioned six years earlier, though pieces of the original road survived as business loops, access roads to the new interstates, and town streets from Chicago all the way to Los Angeles. But the idea of historic preservation was gaining attention in Missouri and other states along the corridor of "America's Main Street."

"We can't give away the story, Grandma," insisted Sam. "Well, a Christmas story, you already know some parts of it--but you'll find out much more Christmas Eve."

"It's going to be an event-filled several days," concluded Louis. "I have," he continued with what he thought a sophisticated rhetorical cough behind a cupped hand, "some significant remarks to make at our Christmas dinner."

"That's wonderful," said his mother. "I'm sure others will want to say something, too."

Inwardly, Louis winced, having anticipated being the one to speak for all. He hoped the idea of many addresses would not spread.

"Leave the Audi under the arch as usual?" Oscar asked his son.

"Yes. You don't need to be out any more in this weather."

Louis liked the idea of a porte-cochère because of its association with aristocracy. Mansions like Buckingham Palace and the White House were designed with carriage porches where residents and guests could enter and depart protected from the weather.

In some ways, he looked forward to the day when the children had all moved out and he and Suzanne would move downstairs into the spacious room at the end of the house. He could park his car under the arch, coming and going through a door no one else used. If he turned the little alcove across the hall into a study, it would be like the CEO's top floor office, accessible only through a private elevator for which one needed a key.

His firm's office building also had its historic character, though it derived more from New World energy than Old World privilege. Ernest Fruehauf immigrated to Missouri early in the 20th century and built a thriving real estate company, Growth Property. Recognizing the potential of a highway carrying families and freight across the country, he became involved in the movement to create Route 66.

Along with influential figures like Cyrus Avery from Tulsa and John Woodruff of Springfield, he lobbied Washington to endorse the first continuous federal highway connecting East and West. Obtaining the easily remembered number 66 was key to the promotion of the new road.

Even before all the aspects of the proposal were approved, Growth Property was buying land along the path where Fruehauf envisioned restaurants, hotels, and gas stations. As more people began to see the business potential of Route 66, he was able to sell lots to individuals and companies, significantly expanding his already substantial wealth. When each new establishment was built, he marked the roadside enterprise he had anticipated with a green pin on a two-state map. They came to look like trees spread along the path of a river.

To mark his own prominence in the city, Fruehauf expanded his office on Manchester Road, adding rounded arches, clusters of columns, recessed entrances, cylindrical towers with conical caps as part of the walls. Unfortunately, he overextended, buying property where he assumed the road would go, only to find the land unstable because of underground rivers, caves wandering into hillsides, faults making earthquake damage likely.

The Romanesque style of his office later appealed to James Morrison, founder of what was now Morrison, Simpson, and Lindbloom, who bought it at auction in 1976.

Louis enjoyed his place in the firm and his spacious third floor office. But even as he swiveled in his high-backed leather chair these days and surveyed the city's skyline through wide windows, he realized that the practice of law was changing faster than he'd like.

While senior partners still made key decisions about cases to take on, legal strategies to pursue, and the deployment of resources, their thinking depended on the exhaustive research done by rising junior members who utilized computers. At times Louis suspected that the next generation was shaping the data, pushing their bosses into options they had determined to be the proper courses.

Several decades ago Louis' father had found changes in government funding altering the kind of research university professors took on. Frustrated at the emphasis on applied science, Oscar developed other interests outside his job and spent less time on publication.

Louis did not have hobbies (other than refining Overton Estate), and he didn't want to be left behind by advances in legal practice. Although he feared another nostalgic review of Oscar's professional career, he might ask his father for advice. Or he could talk to Carol and Mark about computers. But right now he was busy with his role as host.

Late in the afternoon Carol called from Illinois, saying the going would probably be slow tomorrow in the increasingly bad weather. And her brother Curtis phoned from Tennessee to say they had taken the southern route, up from Memphis through Sikeston, but should be in no later than eight that evening.

So, after dinner, all but Sam, Lucy, and Ethel (who were conspiring in the carriage house) adjourned to the family room to wait for Curtis' family. Louis noticed that the way Ben and Liz now viewed their prospects had changed since that day months earlier when Ben sent off his entry photograph and the one-page statement about why he should be selected as the Jimi Hendrix look-alike.

"Benjamin prayed about it, Mr. Lindbloom," Elizabeth said smartly, sipping her coffee. "And God must have heard him. Look at these photos." She pulled a packet from her purse.

Louis had to admit it was eerie. His son had dressed in bellbottom jeans and a leather vest over a long-sleeved T-shirt, teased his hair, and held a borrowed guitar left-handed across his hips. Liz had drawn a slim fake mustache on his upper lip, and his mouth formed an angry scowl. Harry could almost hear the blaring feedback, the wah-wah peddle, the distortion behind the black-and-white images. What words were Jimi/Ben howling?

Suzanne asked, "So God's will is going to grace you with a vacation and a cash prize?"

86

"Stranger things have happened. Remember what the Bible says: "Even the hairs of your head are all numbered. Fear not, therefore; you are of more value than many sparrows.""

Neither parent knew what to say. Although Louis attended church--initially because he was marrying into a Catholic family--he could never take scripture that literally. An investment lawyer, he was used to calculating the odds--profit and loss, management's relationship to the workforce, multi-year track record--and used spreadsheets to predict outcomes. His daughter-in-law's rationale seemed to include wild cards, a personal god intervening to rescue the fortunate.

He also thought about Ben's playing that game, Habitat, on his computer. His avatar or alter ego derived from John Travolta's character in *Saturday Night Fever*, someone unlike Ben, who did not dance well, had been slow to date girls, and enjoyed the social status of St. Louis' wealthy business class. Why did his son want to be someone other than what he was, fortunate son of a very successful St. Louis citizen?

Chapter Fourteen: Worries

The expanded conversation Louis had expected when his brother and family arrived was shorter than he anticipated. The East Coast branch of the family confessed they'd eaten on the road and needed to unpack and get organized. And they wanted to wrap presents now, hoping to find time for one more shopping expedition before Christmas day.

"Of course," Suzanne said agreeably. "You know where you're staying; just ask for help if you need anything."

Louis could see his wife look pointedly at Anne, no doubt hoping that her sister-in-law had persuaded Abigail to join the girls in the converted carriage house rather than stay in a room with Justin. But boyfriend and girlfriend simply joined the larger group headed outside to arrange themselves however they would.

Ben and Liz excused themselves and went to his room upstairs, perhaps to practice being Jimi Hendrix and his girlfriend. Ethel, trailed by Dorothy, followed her grandparents down the hall to tell tales of gathering mollusks in the tidal marshes of Florida. Suzanne and Louis soon found themselves alone in the kitchen as she put away dishes from the evening meal.

"Well, we have plenty of left-overs," she sighed, surveying the packed refrigerator.

"We've also got a gaggle of teenagers who'll eat everything you've cooked. They're obsessed with physical fitness and burn off whatever they take in."

Louis was sensitive about his middle-aged spread, become more pronounced in recent years. Always concentrating on study or work, Louis never seemed to find time to use his own gym or the firm's fitness center. Suzanne let out the clothes he bought in sizes that had fit him five years earlier. And he repressed his doctor's advice to adopt a program of weight loss.

He and his mother were the only ones in the family who had trouble loosing weight once it was on. Carol's military service had mandated regular exercise, which remained a consistent part of her life. Curtis was a recreational runner. And Oscar had always been slender, perhaps because he repressed so much nervous energy.

Louis asked Suzanne, "Did you talk to Ethel about school?"

"Yes, she made Dean's List again this semester."

"As expected. Is she still interested in…what did she call it? 'Biodiversity'?"

"Yes. You understand these things better than I do, but you could also ask Anne."

Louis had read about how rapidly increasing human populations mean rapid loss of plant and animal species. The effects of such changes were beginning to be measured more accurately, and many scientists were warning of massive changes to the environment.

"Boyfriend?" he asked.

"Not the least bit interested. She's like her father, concentrating on her coursework."

Louis, who had always been proud of Ethel's study habits, had lately begun to wonder if her dedication was excessive. Perhaps she should be having more fun at college, branching out to recreational and even romantic activities. When they were in college, Curtis had teased him that he loved no one but Themis (Lady Justice). And a woman carrying a sword and scales, he said, is not a lively companion.

He sighed now. "You know, I always assumed that when the children are grown and out of the house, our worries about them would be over. Now the farther they go and the longer they're gone, the greater my anxiety."

Suzanne wiped her hands on her dishtowel and hung it on a hook by the sink. "I went through this with my younger siblings, wanting them out on their own so that I could finally be out on my own. But I came to realize, when they're with you under one roof, you at least know where they are and what they're doing. So your concern is contained."

She untied her apron, inspected it, and, opening the door to the laundry room, dropped in the dirty bin. "Out of the home," she concluded, "they stretch your desire for their safety and wellness. That's when the church teaches you to trust in God. He keeps the ties strong in a family just as the Father's hand reaches us all wherever we travel."

This was a fine theory, thought Louis; but believing it to the point that you didn't jump at every unexpected phone call was hard to put in practice. Even now he worried about two of his children who were not quite under his roof but out in a separate building. Were they concocting some provocative skit to disrupt at least half the family? Or were they up to even more risky behavior, the kind of thing he read about in the papers?

There had been unsettling discussions in his social circle recently about the explosion of crack cocaine use in America. According to the media, distributors had found they could market the relatively cheap solid, smokeable form and expand their clientele dramatically. Young people from wealthy families, it was said, had the resources to experiment.

He didn't worry about studious Ethel or the son married to the daughter of a brigadier general. But Sam and Lucy, in their impressionable teenage years, went to the best private school in St. Louis, where there was concern about what some called the latest "epidemic." Students were required--and parents encouraged--to attend a series of lectures about the new dangers of addiction. He studied the signs of covert drug use and scrutinized Sam and Lucy's behavior.

Were sudden mood changes evidence of use or just typical teenage insecurity? Was there a window open and the music turned up in the locked bedroom so that smoke could be blown out into the night air? Did weight loss mean increased indulgence? Was "paraphernalia" hidden in their backpacks, the dresser drawers, a garden shed? The more places he considered, the greater his unease.

"They're not using drugs," Suzanne had declared in her usual matter-of-fact way. "You didn't. I didn't. They won't." And she refused to discuss it further.

Suzanne had faith in established structures--schools, churches, courts, legislatures--and especially family. She acknowledged that from time to time faulty individuals caused harm to individuals and groups. But ongoing, moderate reform, she believed, kept society whole, the system running.

The spread of AIDS/HIV in the last decade had also panicked many of the Lindbloom's friends, some of whom stopped volunteering at hospitals. But Suzanne simply followed all the recommended precautions--masks, rubber gloves, vigorous hand washing--and continued to work as a candy striper. Recent news about new treatments for the disease was for her additional conformation that modern civilization was continuing on a steady upward course. More people were more prosperous and healthier and more fulfilled every year.

This conviction, however, was all the more reason not to expect the kind of windfall Elizabeth and Ben were counting on. When Louis and Suzanne went to bed that night, she was ready to talk about their naïveté.

"How can we wake them up about this look-alike fantasy? Ben was doing so well at the bank. It just doesn't seem like him to endorse this crazy idea."

"You know how love is, honey," Louis said. "They're still in that honeymoon stage, and whatever she latches on to, he's bound to join in."

"Well, I'm sure it doesn't seem sensible for her either, especially given the way her father views the world."

Louis agreed. "He doesn't think some miracle will protect the country from danger. I bet he's one of many involved in a deliberate, calculated operation to drive Saddam Hussein out of Kuwait."

"Now, that man is evil," insisted Suzanne. "And he's not going to leave voluntarily, I'm afraid. But that situation isn't what's causing Elizabeth to act the way she is."

"What is then?"

"Didn't you notice that she's more jumpy even than usual on this visit?"

"Racing back out to get mustard?" Louis remembered. "Yeah, that did seem a bit extreme."

"Um-hum. And did you notice that she was always arranging her clothes?"

"Ah, can't say that I did."

92

"Or that she really only pushed her ham and cheese casserole around the plate but then ate both her own and Ben's ice cream?"

That he, like most men, didn't notice these things didn't surprise her, especially because he was focused on being the grand host of the holidays. She was going to give all the pieces, but he had to connect the dots.

"Honey, this means that you're going to find yourself in a new position in this family."

Unfortunately, he had no idea what she meant.

Chapter Fifteen: Voice

While Louis had never gone to any of the Star Wars movies, he had learned many of its famous lines from his children. And, before falling to sleep that night, he heard the phrase, "a disturbance in the field."

His sense of uncertainty in the usually well-organized household increased with the arrival of Carol's family early in the following afternoon. Nieces and nephews, parents and siblings, wife and children (as well as Dorothy the escape artist) were coming and going from room to room, floor to floor, building to building in dizzying combinations.

The twins had been able to kiss the cheeks of everyone as quickly as hummingbirds darting from flower to flower before flying off to the gym with Dorothy, whether to exercise or to play games or practice for "Route 66 to Palestine" Louis didn't know. At least Carol followed them out, as she would be staying in the nearby carriage house. He could only pray that she and Anne would keep reins on the young people and their exuberance.

Mark walked with Oscar to the grandparents' room to quiz him about some electronics matters relevant to his cellular telephone business. In the family room Ben and Justin were involved with Curtis in a discussion of college programs and careers. Louis hoped Ben wasn't promoting look-alike contests over completing an education.

Suzanne, Elizabeth, and Mid began setting up for dinner, a buffet this time, not a sit-down affair: it would not pull all individuals together. Family members would probably wander to different rooms and eat in small groups. Seeing that this entire process was well beyond his control, and thinking about his Far Away, Close to Home story, Louis retreated to his study.

When Thomas Overton, founder and CEO of Flagg Brewery, commissioned an architect for his mansion, he didn't think he needed a study; he ran his business from the office with a minimum of paperwork. But he knew the class to which he aspired would have a private place for the man of the house. So, he told Stephan Grossman to build a small, pentagon-shaped room on the roof at the very center of the house, accessible by an elegant spiral staircase. There Thomas then and Louis now enjoyed a 360-degree view of the grounds but heard none of the commotion from the rest of the estate. In that silence Louis recalled how he once witnessed a single voice commanding an entire auditorium.

A college senior, he'd left his Missouri campus in Columbia and travelled to Madison, Wisconsin, to be a companion for the girlfriend of his best friend's fiancée. Mindy had purchased four tickets to a concert and insisted that she and William double date. And in a strange weekend five hundred miles from home Louis learned something about himself. To convey that truth to his family without embarrassment, however, would involve some artful presentation.

Louis sucked in his breath when he thought about Mindy's friend, Camilla Porter, the girl he always remembered as "she whose beauty knew no bounds." He meant her breasts and her behind, the 'T and A' by which boys measured the value of girls.

Blind dates were traditionally characterized by men through phrases like, "She has a great personality" or "a wonderful sense of humor"--clear warning signs of an unattractive girl. But when Camilla greeted Louis in the dormitory reception area, she took his breath away.

She had a bright smile, laughing eyes, attractively styled auburn hair. But, stunned by the rest of her, he merely registered those features somewhere in the back of his mind. Her young form filled out a white blouse and a tight black mini-skirt as fully as any woman's he'd ever seen. And yet her waist was small, her legs trim, her look athletic.

"Mindy has told me so much about you," Camilla said warmly and shook his hand.

"And...and...I'm so pleased to meet such a good friend of Bill." He'd paid no attention to what he'd been told about her--was she a physics major, a sophomore, from Mindy's home town? He remembered nothing and, in fact, had no desire to fill in her personal history. All he wanted was to get to the right places to admire her...her abundance.

At that time, Louis was trim himself. And though he didn't play any sport beyond table tennis, he had the look of someone naturally fit. Just over six feet tall, with a clear complexion and a serious air, he was found attractive by most girls. His sexual experience, however, was more limited than most in his set.

He knew Camilla couldn't be the girl he was "saving himself for," but she was an immediate challenge to his belief in abstinence. His eyes went wide at the swell revealed when her blouse gapped as they walked across campus. Stepping aside to hold a door for her, his mouth fell open at the sweet bloom of each hip rising and then falling ahead of him. Following her up the auditorium steps, he felt a bulge in his pants. It was amazing, he later realized, that he hadn't tripped over the sidewalk on the way to the hall, bumped into a trashcan, or banged into his seat.

The two couples had arrived twenty minutes before the show was to begin, but the only seats available were high in the back. A sea of heads spread out before and beneath them as they turned to sit. He knew that, for some time after they were settled, his gaze never focused on a single one of the thousand students around him. He simply felt himself located within the aura of an ideal configuration of the female body.

At this time Louis knew little about Joan Baez, the folk music revival, the air of protest that filled campuses more liberal than his own. Bob Dylan, Pete Seeger, and Peter, Paul, and Mary had been drawing huge crowds in many cities, but his taste in music came from his parents. Instead of protests about the war, civil rights, the materialization of American culture, he responded to melodic love songs ("That Old Black Magic") and tunes about exotic places ("Slow Boat to China") from the Big Band era.

Thinking vaguely of June Christie or Ella Fitzgerald, he had expected the soloist he'd come to hear would be performing in an intimate, night-club environment, fifteen or twenty tables crowded around a small stage. He was surprised at the huge space of this university auditorium, row upon row rising in the large doom. Across the expanse in front of and far below him he saw a single tall stool on the stage with a microphone on a stand beside it.

When a slender woman in black walked onstage with her guitar, sat on the stool, and pulled the microphone in front of her, energetic applause was promptly followed by a respectful hush. All eyes and ears turned to that figure and her music.

Joan Baez's voice, as pure and true a sound as Louis had ever heard, seemed to issue from and then rise up and flow out to inspire each listener in the hall. Like everyone else, but unexpectedly, he was mesmerized.

"Oh freedom," she sang, "oh freedom, oh freedom over me / And before I'd be a slave I'll be buried in my grave / And go home to my Lord and be free." Her words expanded and grew stronger and became richer, a magic Louis had never experienced.

The crowd cheered with pleasure at the end of each song, but softly, then stopping to listen to more. Around him Louis could see lips move with the music, fans who knew the words and the melody. Others were still, their mouths open in wonder, admiration, and a kind of love.

So tiny a person, so profound an effect! Louis recognized only a few songs ("Don't Think Twice, it's Alright"), though phrases and refrains were vaguely familiar. He'd probably overheard them on dormitory radios and through open windows in passing cars. But all that sound had been on the periphery, not near the center of his world. It was background noise to his study of government and history, to his plan to become a lawyer, to his drive to achieve a successful, conventional life, fulfilling the expectations of his ancestors.

For a long time, he believed he had been impressed that night by Joan Baez's singing, not by what she sang, the voice not the message. But as years went by, he found his essentially conservative, traditional view of the world had evolved to accommodate some of the sentiments of the radical 1960s. He seldom spoke about these changes in himself, perhaps because his younger brother had endorsed many so completely and his sister rejected most vehemently.

Perhaps, though, now that he thought about it, the occasion for him to put all this into words and share it with his family might just be FACTH. As others talked about travel and discovery, he would conjure up the legendary figure of social activism from his own generation as he had once witnessed her perform. That powerful voice, whose call for hope and change was not inconsistent with the message of this Christmas season, would fill the space of the Overton estate if Thomas could be a capable vehicle.

Camilla Porter and her fabulous body had filled his sexual fantasies for some time; but Joan Baez had taken his heart.

Part 4: Suzanne

Chapter Sixteen: Preparations

As Louis imagined his successful storytelling, Suzanne continued to push away the prospect of revealing anything about herself. She had never wanted to be the center of attention, as a child or an adult. And, less educated than Louis' siblings and their spouses, she didn't feel she had any particular wisdom to offer. She decided to consult her mother-in-law, who often found ways to help her.

Suzanne had learned that Mid had the ability to retain the favor of both sides in a dispute. She could agree with enough of each view to avoid rejecting it, but also voice sufficient reservations to avoid endorsing either. As usual, she would find a path Suzanne could follow.

As she was getting dishes out for dinner, Ben came into the kitchen to say the kids were going to have a snowball fight. He and Liz were volunteering to referee.

"By all means, go," said Mid. "I'm not sure Marian and Christie have ever had the chance in California. But make sure Dorothy doesn't slip out to join them."

Suzanne added, "Sam and Lucy know where the extra galoshes, hats, gloves, and mittens are." Having hosted parties for Louis' firm, the children's friends, and gatherings of her own family, she had made sure the gym had clothes and equipment for every season.

"But tell them," she added, "not to stay out too long in wet clothes. And they'll need to clean up before dinner. That leaves you, Anne, and me," she said to Mid, "to do the cooking."

In her head Suzanne tallied up the combatants soon to be turning her grounds into a battlefield. There were plenty of boys and girls to begin with, but she suspected some parents also would join in the fun. Carol and Curtis, after all, had real military experience and could, she supposed, command opposing armies. She wondered if she should have Louis keep an eye on the game but then remembered men were gravitating toward the library to talk about football.

Although she attended her children's sporting events (soccer, tennis, golf), she had no interest in the games themselves. The endless talk of statistics, records, skills, plays, strategies, players only meant that her husband and children were occupied and generally happy. The discussions sure to dominate this weekend--which college teams would play in what bowls, likely pro teams going to the super bowl, how spring training this year would compare to last, who the prize recruits were--grew to fill men's leisure time but did not add meaning to life.

"Has Carl decided where he might want to go to college?" she asked Anne.

"He'll only say he wants to go where it's warm and far enough from home that we can't keep tabs on him. But we hope he'll widen his search in time."

Listening attentively, Suzanne also reviewed in her mind her decisions about what to prepare for the different likes and dislikes of children (Christie's vegetarianism)) and adults (Elizabeth's sweet tooth), the varied eating practices of families, and the potential changes due to new allergies, health concerns, training regimens.

"It's a good thing you have two ovens," Mid remarked, opening cans of green beans for the casserole she had volunteered to cook. There was also a sizable toaster oven they could use to warm bread. A crock-pot had been cooking vegetable soup since mid-morning.

"The original kitchen was modest, but Louis likes to entertain his clients, so we've expanded the space and the appliances. It's a great convenience because I'm always making things for St. Patrick's or the children's schools and clubs. It's sad only Sam seems interested in learning to cook."

Carol's twins would need lots of protein in their swim regimen, so salmon cakes, one of her best recipes, were on the menu (assuming Christie would eat seafood; she'd ask Carol). Most others would take meat loaf (one had a ketchup and brown sugar topping, one was plain). Louis needed to avoid the starch, so she'd make rice and steer him away from the potatoes. Everyone could add simple green salad, either white or wheat bread, assorted fruit.

Anne looked through a window at snowballs flying, cousins chasing each other, more snow falling. "They're going to work up an appetite. Do we have plenty of dessert besides the angel food cake?" She'd baked it in Virginia and brought it the 800 miles to St. Louis.

"Lucy helped me make cupcakes, and we'll brew a giant pot of hot chocolate, but that reminds me—I assume Carol did bring wine?"

"Oh, yes. Reds, whites, roses, and kinds I've never heard of," laughed Mid. Carol and Mark loved to tour the California vineyards, though carrying their selections on the airplane required some effort. "I think there are enough choices to open our own winery."

Anne asked, "There are refrigerators in the gym and the carriage house, aren't there?"

"Yes. And a freezer downstairs." Suzanne sighed. "Sometimes I feel we don't have a family home so much as a compound."

Anne reflected. "Knowing Louis, I bet there's even a bomb shelter here! Do you remember back when people worried about a nuclear war? They stocked food, water, all the necessities to live underground until it was safe to go out again?"

"Yes," agreed Suzanne. "My family needed all the space we had for my brothers and sisters, sometimes an extra cousin, different grandparents."

Mid mused. "Since the fall of the Berlin Wall, most people think we can leave the apocalyptic mentality behind. I hope that assumption proves correct."

Anne huffed. "Well, if you listen to Carol or Elizabeth, we just have different dangers to worry about. Carol thinks we're on the brink of war in the Middle East, but, even if we were, which I don't believe, that's a long way from our shores."

"Elizabeth tells me, though," said Suzanne, "that Saddam Hussein has biological and chemical agents and could attack us here at home one day if he's not stopped now."

Anne responded, "Well, I'm not about to buy gas masks and stockpile antidotes--if they exist--for whatever disease-carrying weapons they might develop."

Mid: "Carol talks about 'rogue leaders' who won't stop at regional domination. Saddam Hussein took over Kuwait, but won't be content any more than Hitler was before the last war."

Anne: "I know the theory: the more their power at home, the farther they will want it to reach. From Baghdad or Tehran or Pyongyang, individual crazies threaten the entire planet. But I don't want to go to war to stop every little country crossing some border in Africa or Asia or eastern Europe."

Suzanne (sighing): "We may have more serious problems in our own country. They say pollution is limiting fresh air and clear water. Women complain about something they call 'The Glass Ceiling.' Blacks still say they're trapped in poor neighborhoods with weak schools and no jobs. Young people are rebelling against any restrictions established by elders. It's too much for me to understand."

Mid: "It makes me think that the explosions we experienced in the 1960s have spread around the world. It's not always an open revolution, but the status quo is under pressure." She put her casserole in the smaller oven. "But that's something for you and your children to confront. Oscar and I are gracefully conceding our positions of authority."

Suzanne seemed genuinely concerned. "Oh, please don't back away when we need you!"

"At least through this holiday," laughed Anne. "We've got snowball fights, table tennis competition, a story-telling contest all to endure. And a Sergeant of Arms may prove necessary!"

"Speaking of war games," said Suzanne, "would you go make sure all the participants are coming in from the cold often enough to avoid frostbite."

When she was alone with Mid, she confessed, "I need your help on one other matter, Mother."

"One 'other'…Oh, you mean, Abigail and sleeping arrangements. I have an idea on that. But what else?"

"I just don't want to have to do this Far Away Close to Home business. All of you have been out of the country or to distant places in America. But I've lived my entire life in the St. Louis area. And…and…I don't have any profound revelations that would impress the family."

Mid thought a minute. "Didn't you go to Rome once?"

"Oh, as a teenager, in a one-week Easter visit, long ago. We saw the Pope from half a mile away, preaching in Latin in St. Peter's Basilica. I didn't learn a thing."

Mid patted her on the arm. "I don't think that's so. You've always had smart things to say to me, and I'm convinced one of the reasons is your deep faith in the church and in God. Think about it while you cook and clean. I'm sure something will come to you."

And, when she was straightening up after a successful dinner that night, it did.

Chapter Seventeen: Prospects

While Suzanne worked on a story of revelation, she also worried that nothing would change Elizabeth's conviction that she was going to get rich quickly. And then, just after noon on the day before Christmas Eve, Ben received the congratulatory call. Her worse fears were being realized.

Holding the receiver in the kitchen and looking as if he'd been been hit between the eyes with a two-by-four, Ben stood frozen for at least a minute. Then, hanging up, he announced solemnly that he had been chosen by God. "It was not like any voice I'd ever heard over a telephone. It was deep, resonant. I'm sure that the Spirit was talking through him."

It's an advertising company, thought Suzanne. Of course they have trained announcers for such events! They're not likely to leave anything to chance.

Throwing her arms around him, Elizabeth marveled, "There were thousands and thousands of entries. It can't be simple chance that Drew was selected. It's…it's destiny."

The question of destiny took Suzanne back to a childhood friend Jonah, whose destiny might better have been thought of as doom. Twenty years earlier Jonah had told Suzanne innocently, "If there's a bullet over there with my name on it, so be it. When your time comes, it comes."

Now she realized that event was what she had been trying to remember. That was why this whole matter made her so uneasy.

Jonah had come up from Fort Leonard Wood for a last visit with family and friends in St. Louis before shipping out to 1st Engineer Battalion in Da Nang, South Vietnam. They were supporting marines in combat operations throughout the region. As a cook, he told everyone, he could count on being back on the base where the odds of survival were much better than in the bush. ("Of course," he told Louis when Suzanne couldn't hear, "you could still happen to be where a stray rocket or mortar happened to land.)

Several months later he wrote that coming late to a war meant greater chances of getting home safely. With peace talks ongoing, officers didn't want to risk lives. And both North Vietnamese and Viet Cong units, anticipating the U.S. withdrawal, were avoiding major battles. Back in the States and reading the casualty reports, Louis remained skeptical of logic that conveniently guaranteed a happy return to civilian life.

What in the end seemed responsible for Jonah's death was his uncanny physical resemblance to General Creighton Abrams.

Recalling that likeness, Suzanne couldn't help resenting the serendipity Elizabeth was accepting as her due. "God has a plan for Ben, Mrs. Lindbloom," she informed her mother-in-law. She was helping set up card tables in the carriage house so the younger cousins could start a marathon session of Monopoly. "This is the just the beginning. He was meant to win this contest so he could do good work in the world."

Thinking of all the church programs she had worked with all her life, Suzanne asked, "Do you mean he's going to start a charity to help the poor and the destitute?"

"Nothing like that, Mom," Ben explained. "Those efforts, no matter how well meaning, always fail. No, the way to help others is to help yourself. I'm going to start a

108

company that will create jobs. And people who want to lift themselves up can come work for me."

"After our trip, we're going to take the $5,000 prize money and buy a franchise in VitaLife. They sell dietary supplements and homeopathic medicines that have been shown to work, if the customer believes they will."

Suzanne was astounded: her son, a cum laude Ivy League graduate with training in economics, was talking like a high schooler. All she could say was, "So it's a matter of faith, like putting hands on someone?"

"Ben has done that, Mrs. Lindbloom! He cured my sprained ankle with one treatment of VitaRub. Now he can reach out to others. We can run the business even as he works in the bank and I keep up with my studies." She paused. "But, if it goes as the corporation promises, we won't need to."

"You know, Mom," added Ben, "you and Dad could buy in at the ground level, too, and be guaranteed a good return for many years. The more licensed VitaMen we enroll, the larger our network and the greater the profit. You get a percentage of whatever any of your enrollees make in the future. It adds up, I can tell you."

Suzanne knew they would end up at the bottom of a pyramid feeding the few at the top. Of course, she also knew losing their money would be a happier outcome in the long run than they could guess. She decided quietly to seek the advice of others to reign in their foolishness. They should put their check in the bank and continue with their life as it was.

When she next talked to Louis, however, he was unable to focus on that problem, fussing instead about how at the big Christmas dinner both his brother and sister planned to make extensive toasts. They said they wanted to "honor Grandpa and Grandma" who had celebrated their forty-seventh anniversary that year, which was all well and good.

"But it's my house," he complained to Suzanne. "I'm the host, and I should have a chance to address the entire family."

"Oh, you'll have your moment, honey. Let them toast before the meal; you give your address while I serve dessert."

She was putting the ingredients together for two breakfast quiches, one with ham and one with only vegetables, which she would bake and put in the refrigerator. She also had sweet rolls set out on the counter that would rise overnight.

"There's already some friction between Curtis and Carol about the use of the exercise equipment."

"Oh? Surely, there's enough time in the day for everyone."

"Well, Sam told me that his Aunt Carol wants to reserve certain machines for certain times to match the twins' regular regimen--the treadmill and the weight bench especially. But his Uncle Curtis, the college professor who's used to his flexible work schedule, thinks we should be more on a first-come, first-serve system."

Louis tended to resent the freedom academics enjoy, even though Mid had explained that, while college professors might be in class only a dozen hours a week, they ended up working far more than forty hours to meet the publish or perish demands of the profession. Still, Louis felt Curtis and Oscar inflated their hours on the job, counting hours of reflection about their projects, as if other professionals were at work only when they punched a clock.

110

"Could you get your father to devise a schedule with mostly free times, but some reserved sessions for Christie and Marian? He loves to draw up schemes like that."

"Oh, he'll draw one up for you--or five of them. But each proposal will be more complex than the last as he plots variables like 'expanded meal times,' 'vacation sleep patterns,' 'women's monthly cycles.' The theory will be highly entertaining, but practical application will be vague at best."

No matter how many luxury facilities Louis added to the estate, thought Suzanne, there always seemed a need for more. When the gym was being designed, Suzanne had lobbied for a swimming pool. Recently, she'd thought it would be good for Louis, controlling weight and the stress he seemed to be feeling despite his many successes in life. And right now it would have have relieved the battle for access to exercise equipment.

"Well," she told Louis, "I hate to put another burden on your mother, but I don't know who else can resolve this." She paused. "Oh, and there is the preparation for 'Route 66 to Palestine,' which would have to be factored in to any schedule."

"You mean Sam has mandated a series of rehearsals for the skit?"

"I'm afraid to ask him, as after each session with his sisters and cousins, he says they need to more research, have to revise some parts, want to work on costumes. I'm almost afraid to think how this is going to turn out."

Suzanne was happy to have diverted Louis' attention away from the question of who would get to speak when. She was sure, so long as he went last, his would be the remarks that stayed in everyone's mind. But she didn't anticipate that her older son Ben would confess to a secret.

And the others would have to reshape their remarks in relationship to an unexpected (but also expected) event.

Chapter Eighteen: Chains

The next morning, Christmas Eve, Suzanne had yet one more reason for anxiety when Mark teased his brother-in-law, Curtis. "How about those 'environmental extremists,' " he joked. "Those 'liberals' value the spotted owl over development that meant economic prosperity for the people of California."

Cutis knew Mark was just "pulling his chain," as Justin would phrase it; but he couldn't let the matter go without raising a modest objection. "The timber industry has already destroyed 90% of old forests in the Pacific Northwest, my friend. There are other ways to create jobs and opportunities. Your own cellular phone business, for instance, is expanding rapidly. It's employing thousands of young people without having to cut down a single tree."

Suzanne had brought orange juice, cereal, and pastry out to the gymnasium for those who didn't want a hot breakfast. Ethel started coffee brewing at the little bar beside the mini-refrigerator.

"To tell the truth, we cut down some trees to build transmission towers," Mark pointed out. "But timber can be replanted, forests restored. It's a crazy bunch of tree-huggers that has caused the trouble--as if we don't have enough real worries in this country. The spotted owl! Species go extinct all the time. It's law of nature you people need to learn to accept."

Curtis laughed. "Well, I'm not sure who 'we people' are, exactly. But you need to understand that the owl is like a canary in a coalmine--an indicator of the state of the area. If he stops singing, it's because something bad has happened to him and will soon happen to the miners. Gas, probably, or lack of oxygen."

Suzanne nodded meaningfully at her daughter, hoping she would be able to moderate the discussion, "Coffee, gentlemen?" asked Ethel politely, holding up a full cup.

"That doesn't apply in California," Mark insisted. "The government has decided the owl's 'an endangered species' in Oregon and Washington, but for us it's only a 'threatened species.' The nature lovers are fudging the definition in order to expand their power base. They want to run the whole country."

"Well, there is nature all over the country, so, yes, I guess they want to protect all the land that sustains us. Thanks, sweetie," Curtis said to his niece.

"You're welcome," she smiled. "And, not to complicate things even more here, but we have to worry about our water as well as our land. "

"Uh-oh. The younger generation heard from," said Mark, smiling at Suzanne.

"I am studying marine biology, as you know. And it's a bit frightening how intensive agriculture in coastal regions is affecting not just our rivers but the oceans they feed."

"Scientists are finding new ways to purify water as fast as modern industry expands to feed our people. You can't have a prosperous country without enough food for workers."

Suzanne asked Ethel, "Didn't you explain to me how it's not just the spotted owl that's threatened by loggers?"

Ethel hiked a hip up to sit on the third stool at the counter. "The owl is an indicator of the health of all living

114

things in that system. At the top of the food chain, if it's not finding enough to eat, that means the number of smaller birds and rodents is dwindling because they can't forage what they need to survive. And humans depend on the same systems for their existence."

Mark threw up his hands in mock exasperation. "Who can argue with young people? And we're just trying to make sure they can have a good life after we're gone."

"Let's work off our frustration at a game of ping pong," suggested Curtis. Suzanne was happy to see this mostly friendly discussion come to an end.

She was less happy that afternoon when her brother-in-law had to abandon a second argument with less resolution. Suzanne had asked Curtis to use his skills as an educator to open Ben and Elizabeth's eyes on the look-alike contest.

"I think I understand why this appears to be a great opportunity," Curtis began. Suzanne had invited them all to her sewing room for this conference. "But let me review what's happened so far to make sure I have the right ideas. I mean, it all starts with Jimi Hendrix, right? If he hadn't become famous, there wouldn't have been a contest, you wouldn't have won, and you wouldn't have the money to buy into VitaLife."

Ben admitted, "Yes, though it's possible I might resemble a different celebrity..."

"Well, okay, agreed."

Suzanne folded her hands in her lap and tried to look relaxed. She'd had to confront her other children at various times, but Ben had been so like his father—following the rules, accepting conventional wisdom—that it had never been necessary in his case...until now.

Curtis went on. "As it is, though, God's plan for you begins with Jimi Hendrix, a rock music sensation whose performance inspired a whole generation. And, of course, he--or his agent or his producer or his record company--made millions of dollars on his talent. And that legacy made the look-alike contest possible. People he made rich put on this event, and you became another benefactor of his fame and fortune, if a small one."

Elizabeth interrupted, "Mr. Lindbloom, you should know these things happen all the time. People become famous, and their lives affect all sorts of people they never knew."

"Yes, I do see that." Curtis rubbed his chin, and Suzanne nodded. "Still, I can't quite think Jimi Hendrix played music just so you would receive a surprise cash gift one day 40 years after this death. Did you know, by the way, that he was in the Army?"

"The Army? I wouldn't have thought that."

"God does work in mysterious ways, I guess. One might even say his later success was inspired, at least in part, by his military service. You see, he was given a choice, after getting into some trouble as a youngster: prison or the Army. It was 1961, no war on the horizon--well, none that he could see--so off he went."

Suzanne had warned him not to mock the young people's logic and hoped he wouldn't ask if it had been God's will that Hendrix had been caught riding in stolen cars; or if had been ordained that the single way to stay out of prison was life in the military; or if his weeks at Fort Campbell, Kentucky, were providential, meant to strengthen his faith. She knew Curtis' sarcasm could be sharp, and the tone of a discussion with Elizabeth might escalate sharply.

To keep a broad perspective, she offered, "In those days all the men were subject to the draft, if they were healthy. The only question was which branch and how long."

Curtis agreed. "That was true for my generation, sons of the WWII vets; we all expected to go in. Ben, your father, was lucky with the lottery, but not everyone was."

Suzanne believed Curtis did not envy his brother's escape from the draft. He told her that those who were spared his war would do much for society as civilians.

"You realize what 'universal' conscription means when you see the new recruits like yourself in formation. Their heads are shaved, and they're wearing identical stiff new fatigues. They look amazingly alike."

Suzanne knew her father-in-law's story about pre-induction physicals and smiled--amazingly alike from other perspectives.

Elizabeth said, "I'd like to think some stand out as individuals, not just duplicates of an archetypal GI Joe." Suzanne knew she was thinking about her father, a high-ranking officer.

"True, some don't fit in," continued Curtis. "Jimi was one. He couldn't make it without his music, lost with no guitar. So, after awhile, his father shipped it across the country to him."

"Fathers do take care of their children," smiled Ben.

"It was a nice gesture by Mr. Hendrix, Sr.--sending the guitar; but it may have hurt more than helped. Playing his music, you see, Jimi neglected his duties and eventually had to leave the Army--'unsuitability,' was the official reason. He was lucky in some ways, though. He had already finished paratrooper training. If he'd stayed in, he might have been killed in Vietnam."

Elizabeth huffed. "Well, he went on to a great career. This was just a bump in the road to a success that was meant to be."

"Perhaps success, but then disaster. You know how unscrupulous promoters and slick agents take advantage of people when they become famous, when they have some money. They made sure Jimi had a ready supply of alcohol and drugs. He died of an overdose in 1971--about the time I was in overseas."

Suzanne gave an involuntary shiver. That was also the time Suzanne's classmate Jonah had died in Vietnam.

Chapter Nineteen: Links

Suzanne received good news from her mother-in-law. "Abigail is staying with the other girls in the carriage house," Mid informed her as they were cleaning up after lunch on Christmas Eve. Suzanne had been reluctant to ask.

"Oh, that's wonderful, Mother. Thank you. How ever did you persuade her?"

Mid folded the dishtowel and laid it over the rack beside the sink. "Actually, I let her come to her own conclusions. But I prepared the way by talking about my service in the Red Cross during the war."

"Louis has told me that you took food to the troops, but he didn't know exactly what you did, where you did it, why you volunteered in the first place." Suzanne pulled a chair out from the little kitchen table and gestured for Mid to sit. She refilled her glass from a pitcher of ice tea.

"I never really talked about it with the boys. They wouldn't have been interested, but Carol was curious." She sighed. "You know, I've begun to think recently that what I told her may have inspired her to enlist twenty some years ago."

Suzanne nodded. "It never ceases to amaze me how some little thing we say to our children later turns out to be the inspiration for their style of dress or their choice of career or where they want to live or even…even who they fall in love with."

Suzanne was proud of Ethel's commitment to the field of marine biology, but she believed it would mean she must always live far from her Missouri home…and from her children's grandmother. More than once Suzanne had wondered if having taken her daughter, at age eight, to an exhibit on whales at the St. Louis Zoo was the inspiration for the course her life was taking. Throughout that one three-hour tour Ethel's mouth was open in amazement. And from that single experience, it seemed, she had built in her head a lifetime of travel and study around the globe.

Mid filled her tea glass. "I think I do better now--when it probably doesn't matter!--in shaping what I say to children and grandchildren. That is, I used to just be unburdening myself about whatever worried me or something I'd been happy to discover. I simply spilled it all out. Now I consider my audience more carefully and and try to calculate how they will react to what I say and how I say it."

Suzanne thought about her efforts to steer Ben away from believing in windfalls. She'd probably done what Mid had learned not to do--spoken her piece straight from her heart rather than figuring out how to get the reaction she wanted.

"I would have thought your going overseas would encourage Abigail to be independent, do what she wanted rather than do what was expected."

"It's true that I surprised my family when I told them I would be delivering donuts to soldiers in the field. They believed I should continue to wait for the man of my dreams. The single moment of our meeting, they believed, would lead me to the life my sisters were already enjoying--a home, children, stability."

"Weren't you in danger, too? One moment might collapse your whole future!"

"We don't need to talk about that," said Mid, rising to put her glass by the sink. "What I explained to Abby was the unexpected camaraderie we felt in our Clubmobile. The idea of a 'sisterhood' wasn't fashionable then the way it would be later, in the 1960s and afterwards. But the girls in our unit formed relationships independent of men that we'd never known were possible. And we were in charge of our own mission--we loaded supplies, we made dough, we cooked in hot oil. Well, and I drove and repaired a truck!"

"Ah," sighed Suzanne, rising. "So Abigail will be with Christie, Marian, Lucy, Mary Anne, and probably Ethel, a new band of sisters…or female cousins."

"She didn't say that exactly, but a certain distance from Justin, an allegiance with others in his family, seemed to appeal to her." Mid got up, too, and they returned to their work.

Suzanne wondered if could she fashion a tale that would get Ben--well, Elizabeth first, she supposed--to see that steady application in a good field was a better guarantee of satisfaction than a money-making scheme that depended on gullible customers.

The couple's illusion of magical rescue from the struggle to achieve a meaningful life reminded her again of Jonah, her high school friend who had believed he would be lucky in Vietnam and come home a hero. He had, Suzanne understood, looked the part.

Jonah had prematurely grey hair and wore it in a crisp military cut. His stout physique and square jaw made him look like a leader, even more like an officer than a sergeant. Suzanne had a hard time, however, accepting the theory his family endorsed, that a sniper had mistaken him for the commander of allied forces in all of Vietnam.

Louis had explained to her, "The enemy wants to take out commanders, so a unit's CO might not be positioned at the head of a formation, a primary target." While he remained relieved that he would not have to go to war, he'd read widely about what it was like over there. "They say that the life expectancy of second lieutenants in combat is less than 30 minutes."

Thinking of Jonah's false sense of security, Suzanne decided to follow up on Curtis' story of Jimi Hendrix with Ben and Liz. As she wrapped presents before her family would leave for midnight mass on Christmas Eve, she brought the subject up again. All her children were in the library to help, but Elizabeth was sitting beside her.

"Let me make these bows a bit more…more attractive," Liz told Suzanne, undoing one and beginning to refashion it in a more complex pattern.

"Please do," said Suzanne. "I'm not an artist. I bought this bag of bows and ribbons on sale after last Christmas."

"I love origami, and I've created a number of distinctive patterns for special occasions."

Suzanne said. "You're artistic, I know. You have that temperament--that everything should be just so. Plain old people like me…well, we accept some things the way they are."

"Um-hm. Hand me those little scissors, would you?" Suzanne slid the scissors across the table and pulled a short piece of scotch tape off the roll. "I think of poor people like Jimi Hendrix, who couldn't accept the way things are. He played the guitar like no one ever had! It's so sad his career ended in tragedy."

"Oh, I wouldn't call it a loss. His music survives, and he's influenced later musicians."

"Yes. And I have to admit there are a lot of stories like Jimi's--the money and attention go to the heads of the star born overnight and they lose all perspective." She took up another present, a book on exercise and staying fit for Louis. "Still, though, I'm trying see the Holy Spirit at work in all this--Jimi's time in the Army, the music, the war, the tours, the industry. It must lead to more than early death. Good is supposed to come out of evil, so maybe your good fortune was in the making for half a century."

She snapped off another piece of tape to hold down the folded paper.

"It is kind of a high price to be paid, though, when you think about it, to take you two to Las Vegas. I sometimes wonder a lot about what happened to Ben's Uncle Curtis--you know, being drafted--'selected,' as it were, by Selective Service--going to Vietnam, and surviving. I don't think God needed all those other men, on both sides, to be chosen by death. But it does make me reflect sometimes--and be grateful that he was spared."

Elizabeth scowled. "God doesn't make wars, men do. It happens all the time in the Bible. People stray from the faith, and they're punished."

"Yes, the Jews were sent into exile. But was every one corrupt? Are all the men and women who died in Vietnam…or those who might die if we go to war against Saddam--evil? Were their deaths necessary so that God could show the rest of us the errors of our ways?"

Suzanne recalled the story of General Abrams' morale-boosting tour to units in I Corps. Calculating that the enemy would be unable to mount any kind of attack in the region at this point, the Army publicized the trip widely. Back home--and around the world--the General was seen getting out of helicopters in jungle villages, shaking hands with men in mess halls, telling subordinates in sandbagged headquarters' buildings that peace was near at hand.

Jonah's CEO had all the men's names put in a helmet, and he drew out two who would have the good fortune to be among those greeting the general when he visited a firebase near the coast. Due to a mix-up, Jonah and the other man were flown in at the same time the General was expected. The first man off the chopper, Jonah was dropped by a sniper's single bullet fired, they claimed, from a quarter of a mile away. He had only a week left in his tour.

Suzanne felt—and she was right—that there would be a moment like that in this holiday—when the unexpected would take them by surprise.

Chapter Twenty: Sparrows

Suzanne had learned about the Vietnam war indirectly. Although she had older cousins in the military, no one in her family had been sent there. In church announcements and in the St. Louis paper she saw notices of local soldiers killed, wounded, or missing in action. So Jonah became for her the embodiment of those anonymous casualties.

The two young people had not been close friends in their school years, but the families, members of the same church, knew each other. And there had been one, unrepeated semi-flirtatious exchange between the upper-class boy and the younger girl.

A few years later, when Louis was dating Suzanne, he met Jonah at a church supper where they learned they were both fans of Big Band music. When he came back to St. Louis that final time, Suzanne gave up a ticket so he could go with Louis to hear Duke Ellington's orchestra.

After the news of his death spread through the parish, Suzanne began to recall experiences they'd shared in school--ninth grade geometry--and at church--an effort to establish an international club. She found it odd that she and Jonah had been at the same places many times, but it had never registered that they were in some senses connected.

The more her memory roamed over recent years, though, the more his rugged face, his strong figure took a place in many scenes. She knew she was scanning the past with a selective lens, yet it seemed he continued to show up in spaces she had thought were occupied by others or were simply empty.

She was positive that he had not been on the trip to the Vatican she had taken with a dozen other young people from the diocese, but as Ben's look-alike contest had brought back memories of Jonah, she felt he was in her mental pictures as she tried to compose a Far Away Close to Home story. He was just out of sight behind that pillar, or in the shadows of this shop awning, or with the group turning a corner in the airport concourse. In retrospect this Christmas, he began to haunt the most intense religious experience of her life.

More mature looking than his peers, Jonah was noticeable in crowds. Outgoing, humorous, though not particularly attractive to most girls, he made friends easily and enjoyed group activities. He was also a good athlete (football and wrestling) and was recruited by local universities before graduation. Suzanne saw him as very much above her.

They'd had only one exchange that she remembered. He was the leader of the team asked to construct a church float for the Easter parade; and Suzanne was assigned to help create the scene--Mary Magdalene speaking to the two angels at Jesus' tomb.

Jennifer Porter and Betty Simms, both talented artists, had shaped the forms in wire mesh attached to two-by-four post supports. Suzanne's job was to fold up colored tissue paper into clusters that could be poked into the mesh and simulate Mary's flowing robes.

"Mary Magdalene looks as much like an angel as the angels," noted Jonah, looking at the three figures. Having cleaned up the flatbed truck onto which they would put the sculptures, he was wiping his hands on a rag. "You'd better bring her down to earth a bit, don't you think?"

Suzanne had copied the technique used by Jennifer and Betty and hadn't emphasized the different natures of

126

angels and mortals. "You're right!" she laughed. "Why don't you give her a hug, and some of whatever's all over you will make her more human?"

He inspected his hands, which were still stained by grease and dirt. "I could give you a hug, too, but the hay in your hair and the dye that's come off the tissue paper onto your fingers--and your nose--already have you looking like an earthly creature."

She blushed, unsure whether this was another joke or something more. "Well, we in our right roles, then, for now."

A better solution for the Mary sculpture turned out to be some off-white spray paint that created shadows in her clothes and a bit of charcoal to darken the areas below her eyes on the papier-mâché head.

Later, as she was watching the parade float ride by with Jonah as a Roman guard at the back, Suzanne saw him look at Mary, then at her, then at Mary, then at her, and wink. There were no later references to the scene or their implied places in it; but that Jonah had spotted her among the many spectators along the road that day made her feel important.

She would not, however, insert him into her tale for the family. She would also omit an account of the process by which she was selected for the trip to Rome. Each of the churches in the St. Louis area nominated a young person distinguished by service to others. A wealthy parishioner in the diocese had donated the funds to cover all expenses for the trip.

Suzanne had done what she'd done--teaching children, working in the kitchen, taking part in charity drives--by instinct, not with a desire to be recognized. She had absorbed Catholic teaching without finding it contradictory to her own nature; so she had been surprised at the selection. Now she felt it inappropriate to explain that process in her FACTH. She would simply tell how the trip confirmed what she thought she'd known all along.

The journey from her home to the St. Louis airport, to NYC, to London, to Rome had been dizzying. She and her fellow teenagers were guided (and chaperoned) by four parents and two priests, taken up to counters, across lobbies, down concourses, through gates, into cabins. Often in the middle of the party, Suzanne felt protected but also restrained.

At the airport, she was packed into a bus with her fellow pilgrims and rode at night in a light rain down narrow, twisting streets to a youth hostel. Sharing a room with three other girls, she had a fitful night of semi-sleep and then was once more wedged in among her companions on a tour bus that carried them to a drop off point near their destination.

Fog and drizzle followed them through passageways and between buildings for half an hour and then through a final series of turns and twists into St. Peter's Square. She could feel the cobblestones beneath her feet but would not realize the extent of the pavement until later. When the fog lifted, the tall granite obelisk rose in the center of the milling crowd. And above the heads of people close to her the colonnades encircling the square became visible.

The skillfully amplified sounds of the mass reached her party, and they found places to stand. Within the throng of worshipping Christians, Suzanne felt secure, strengthened, connected to a worldwide community. But not to God.

Throughout her church education she'd been told she was always watched over by the Father, that God knew her and her life journey from the beginning of time to the

128

end of human history. But standing in the vast space of St. Peter's Square, she had to believe she was so insignificant that not even the omnipotent would spot her.

"How could He know I'm here?" wondered the fifteen-year-old child. "I'm six thousand miles from everything that makes me who I am. Here I'm a tiny speck in a vast sea of people in the city of Rome in the country of Italy, the continent of Europe, the other side of the world. And there are millions more worshipping Christ around the globe. There is nothing about my being or history that would lead God to me."

Even her fellow pilgrims from Missouri, she felt, had lost their individuality among the masses and so far from home. Their names and histories had been erased after a grueling twenty-hour journey and in the enormity of the space they now shared, by the sheer numbers of individuals hearing the same words over the loud speakers, within the myriad voices reciting in unison age-old expressions of faith.

Then Suzanne thought about the past, the numbers of believers who had gathered to worship in churches and cathedrals or prayed alone in closets or barns or fields. In this very spot alone, she knew, millions of the faithful had stood and had identical thoughts. She was consumed in the timeless repetition of human desire and suffering, eternal hope and fear, endless longing and regret--a look-alike to uncountable others.

But God the Father as she'd pictured him, was remote--an image in stained glass windows, a picture in a Sunday school book, drawings in crayon by children. Within her family and the familiar environment of her regular life she'd known God in church services, in charitable acts, in small gestures of kindness. Where was He now?

Still, she admitted she was not, she could not be, anyone but herself. Forces far greater than herself had carried her from a simple home and ordinary family around the world to stand before God. Yes, she was different from everyone else; but she was known by God in the same way all of us are. She was one soul created in God's likeness working to refine the divine within to serve in His Kingdom now and forever. Amen.

Interlude: Palestines

"Did I tell you about the woman we met at the Raleigh-Durham Airport this spring?" Curtis asked me a few months after his son's wedding. We were taking a break from his transcription of volume four of my family history.

"You didn't mention anyone in particular. Was it someone you knew, an old friend?"

"No, a complete stranger, but your recalling the Christmas play, 'Route 66 to Palestine,' reminded me. It's about travelers caring for their family on a long journey."

Now that he's been retired for a few years, Curtis has taken on a number of new causes: preserving Route 66 and supporting military families, for instance. Since the Mother Road didn't pass through North Carolina, I guessed his story had something to do with veterans. "A mother, father?"

"Well, at first I didn't know. What happened was that Anne, the animal lover, got to chatting with a woman in the waiting area by the gate. This other lady, quite a bit younger, had a small dog with her in a bright red traveling case. 'She's been with me all over the world,' the woman said proudly. 'She's a great companion.'"

"Ah, perhaps a Chihuahua like Pearl?" I gestured at the four-pound pet that was sniffing around my living room. Curtis and Anne were keeping her for six weeks while Justin and Isabella took an extended honeymoon on the other side of the world.

"No, but not much bigger. One of those tiny spaniels, I think. Anyway, the dog rode in a soft cage but was well-enough behaved to be allowed to sit on her owner's lap, have a biscuit, and drink water from her own little cup."

"So, it's like the baby Jesus Ethel carried in a basket for the play."

Twenty some years ago, the children's holiday drama had the Joad family riding in a rundown pick-up truck along Route 66 during the Depression. It was Christmas Eve, and they were trying to find a place to spend the night on their way to California, which they thought of as the promised land. The baby was Dorothy, Louis' little dog.

"Yes," laughed Curtis. "But this traveling pet wasn't like Dorothy, the escape artist! For 'Route 66 to Palestine' Sam had to tie her to the basket, she'd gotten away so many times."

"Right! She kept turning up in the manger scene-- well, the cardboard Hooverville shelter Marian and Christie put together."

"She'd made the carrier her den. Anyway, at the Raleigh airport it turned out this traveler's first flight—on her way from North Carolina to Alaska—had been canceled after she'd arrived at the airport. She had been all checked in at 10:00 in the morning but, in order to reschedule, had to go back though security with the dog and all her baggage."

"That's too bad. But it at least gave her the chance to walk her dog in an approved area, which you might need to do right now." I pointed at Pearl, whose sniffing seemed suspicious.

"You're probably right!" he said, jumping up. "We'll take a break and be right back."

The Chihuahua was not completely house trained, I fear. Her home in Mexico was on a rocky hillside, three flights up. So getting her out and finding a grassy spot in time to avoid accidents had been a challenge for my grandson and his bride.

Thinking of Justin and Bella on the other side of the American continent made me realize that "Route 66 to Palestine" seemed in retrospect a reflection of my family's diaspora, children and grandchildren journeying far from home. When my generation traveled overseas, they generally imagined coming back home to stay, as the GI's did in World War II. The next generation, though, considered living abroad more seriously. And their children see the whole world as one place in which to live. Some, I've read, even consider outer space to be part of the human territory!

"Success!" Curtis announced as he came back in. Pearl, apparently satisfied with her brief walk, was dancing at his feet, wanting to be picked up so she could sit on his lap. He continued his story. "The woman and her dog were eventually re-booked on an afternoon plane; and with the new boarding pass in hand, she endured the process of having herself and her effects screened a second time. Now she was waiting for the same plane on which we had seats."

"Didn't you say she was going to Alaska? She must have had several stops ahead of her in that journey; and her day had already included obstacles."

Curtis sighed. "We didn't know how many. You see, encouraged by Anne's interest, she eventually revealed that she was the wife of an Army sergeant--seven years in the service, three tours in Afghanistan. He had been wounded (lost part of a hand), experienced several concussions, was perhaps developing a need for counseling, but was reluctant to seek it."

"That's where she was headed? To rejoin him? It sounds like he needed her."

"Very much so. But then we learned that she needed him, too. After his most recent time overseas, she had been unwell on and off for several months. In Fairbanks, after a battery of tests, she was tentatively diagnosed with MS, the symptoms of which, as you know, include tiredness, tingling in the limbs, vision problems. And they're often augmented by stress."

Anne's sister had lived with this disease for over forty years, and in the last decade or more of her life she'd been cared for by Anne in Rustic—another reason, besides having a husband who'd been in the Army herself, Anne would be sympathetic to this traveler.

Curtis continued. "Over the last few weeks, she'd been to see a specialist near her parents. They could help with the children who were with her while the mom underwent tests at the hospital. A few days ago, her physical condition was confirmed and a treatment plan established. Now she was returning to care for her family."

"The importance of family," I noted. "Grandparents and parents."

"So true. Anyway, overhearing this conversation, I offered to get my wife a soft drink and asked the mother if she'd like something also. She thanked me and began unpacking her purse to find some money. I waved her off, saying she and her family had done enough for me and mine."

"Good for you. Too often these days the gestures of support we make for the troops and their families are kind of anonymous. We watch a parade, put flag stickers on our bumpers and pins in our lapels. But we don't have much to do with the soldiers themselves."

"It later occurred to me that I might have done more." He rubbed Pearl's head.

Since two of my three children served in the military, we're generally sensitive to how the nation rewards their sacrifice.

"When our flight was called, she got up, gathered her dog and her travel bag, and came over to exchange a hug with my wife. An hour and a half earlier, they were complete strangers. I'm sure she appreciated Anne's sympathy. The long journey ahead would stretch into the next day at least; and when she arrived home the real hard work of family would begin."

While my children and grandchildren are now on three—or is it four?—continents, I'm proud to say we have always responded to each others' needs no matter how far the distance that separates us. The sense of commitment to each other was strengthened at our 1990 Christmas gathering, which did have complications.

"Do you remember how the power went out in the middle of the children's play?" I asked Curtis.

"Of course. Great dramatic effect! We all assumed it was the snow bringing down power lines, but it was still a shock when the room went dark."

I smiled because I was the only one of the grownups in on the plot within the plot.The lights going out had been part of the grandchildren's play. The boys were electronics wizards, so in addition to sound effects there was an elaborate system of lights set up in the gymnasium.

"We should have known your brother would have a backup generator on the premises." Curtis smiled. "The staging was so good, we didn't think about what caused the blackout, or how the lights came back on."

The only place the Joads in "Route 66 to Palestine" could find to spend the night was one of our famous Missouri caves. We were supposed to imagine going into the darkness with them. And just then, that's what we had: darkness.

The military spouse in the Raleigh-Durham airport must have felt some light come into her life when she met my son and daughter-in-law. To those not aware of her burdens that day she was just one more traveler, deserving no exemptions from policies governing the care of pets and those traveling with pets—she had to have papers, identification, tickets. For a few moments in the waiting area, though, she was with two people who understood her plight outside such documentation.

Curtis sighed. "You know, if I'd had my wits about me. . . they were scattered by the matter-of-fact way the young mother spoke about all she was going through…if I'd been thinking at all, I would have made sure she was booked first-class for the rest of her journey."

Part 5: Curtis

Chapter Twenty-one: Births

Ten minutes after the (shower) curtain fell on "Route 66 to Palestine," pandemonium broke out. Fortunately, the teenagers were celebrating their dramatic success in the gymnasium and weren't aware—at the time, at least—of the dissension among the grownups.

Louis would be convinced that Elizabeth had inaugurated the uproar when she claimed that Mary Anne hadn't been holding the fictional baby (Dorothy) correctly. Carol jumped to her niece's defense in her typically blunt military style, causing Elizabeth's back to stiffen. Then, making more than one set of eyes roll, Oscar began a short but complex discussion of forces, vectors, and inertia that "proved" there were many correct ways to hold a baby.

Anne interrupted her father-in-law and tried to calm everyone by saying they were missing the point of the play and the holiday—good news, charity, hope. "We're all going to church tonight or tomorrow," she said. "Let's not mix up the trivial with what's truly important."

The idea that his wife's complaint had been unimportant led Ben to blurt out that he was offended anyone would criticize his Elizabeth on this subject, "...when...when," he stuttered, "we're the ones who're expecting a baby."

There was silence. Mark rallied with an awkward congratulations, and then came the usual questions about due date, the parents' plans, how everyone could help. But they understood that their grand family gathering was encountering an expected challenge to harmony.

When Curtis asked how long she'd known, Elizabeth hemmed and hawed. Quickly Mid hugged the mother-to-be and blurted, "What does it that matter when we're learning that Elizabeth's expecting! This is the family's first grandchild, so we're all expecting!"

Elizabeth paled. She'd told her own parents about the pregnancy (and the gender) weeks ago, unconsciously thinking of them as *the* grandparents. Her conscious mind understood that she and her children were also "Lindblooms"; but she had and would always think of herself as a Stafford. And that was the family into which James would be born.

"Elizabeth, here, sit down," Suzanne urged. "You don't look well. All this excitement is upsetting you." She had been the only one to suspect her daughter-in-law's condition. "The rest of you, fix yourself a drink, please. We need some time to absorb this wonderful news."

Suzanne's suggestion muted discussion. The topic, however, would resurface—sometimes forcefully— throughout the remainder the holiday. For the moment, though, the ramifications of the news—and the suspicion that it had been deliberately kept from them—were matters talked over quietly in small groups.

Curtis took the issue up with Anne the next afternoon as he was inspecting his Christmas presents—the shirts, ties, books, and jigsaw puzzles that represented a life he already had. "Well, it seems to me that we—we who are *not* expecting to be grandparents any day soon—might need to find some new hobbies."

"Aren't we busy enough," Anne said, "working full-time and raising kids? We've got a few years before contracting the 'empty nest' syndrome." She was folding wrapping papers, rolling up ribbon, stacking boxes to save for next Christmas.

The different groups within the family had been to their various church services the night before or early this morning. After lunch had come the frenzy of unwrapping, ooh-ing, and ah-ing. Ben had reported that Elizabeth was feeling a bit unwell—"you know, the morning thing"— and was resting. By now the news had reached everyone, surprising even Ben's siblings. No one had seriously thought about the arrival of a next Lindbloom generation.

Curtis chuckled. "You know, I think Louis' jaw hit the floor when he heard the news."

"A grandchild on the East Coast—that probably wasn't in his plan."

Curtis slid his shirts into a single bag. "I keep reading how people our age are going to have an expanded lifespan. Good diets, regular exercise, and medical advances mean we'll live decades into our retirement. That's a lot of years we need to fill up with more than grandkids."

"'Fill up'? You're thinking of our Golden Years as some gigantic warehouse we have to cram to the top with memorabilia?" She paused thoughtfully. "But you're right that we're staying active longer. There are women my age giving birth, you know."

Curtis' jaw fell. "Hey! We've had our allotment, plus one," he said. "But there's no reason we can't start taking up...oh, I don't know..." He waved his arms expansively. "...snow skiing or scuba diving or building and flying our own gliders. But we need to get started with these activities before our employers present us with institutional rocking chairs."

"Aren't you going to announce at dinner tonight that we hope to buy waterfront property? That'll provide activities for a lot of weekends and summers."

140

"Now that you mention it, learning to sail would be a fine thing." Curtis had a sudden, inspiring vision of himself restoring old boats, designing and building his own craft, maybe going into business one day with a son…and/or a grandson.

She gestured toward the window, perhaps to change the subject. "I hope the weather will clear up a bit. I'd like to go out to Times Beach."

"The village where all the chemicals were used? It's a ghost town, as I understand it."

"I've read about what happened. But I'd still like a first-hand view for when I teach environmental science next semester." Her teaching and research had been reinvigorated by the nation's growing understanding of water and air pollution.

Curtis admitted, "Hmm. I might be interested in Times Beach as a commentary on the American Dream. It's right on Route 66, you know. Well, where the road used to be."

"Yes. According to what I've learned, the town was built to offer St. Louis residents convenient summer homes. Only twenty miles west of downtown and on the Meramec River."

"One of those American real estate schemes—cheap land then, but as the city expanded out that way, its value would increase. Ten, fifteen years later, you sell at a nice profit."

"Unfortunately, twenty years ago, to keep the dust down in dry weather, they started spraying oil on their streets. But the oil, contaminated by residue in the trucks that brought it in, contained toxic levels of dioxin."

"Ah, the good stuff we sprayed for deforestation in Vietnam."

To eliminate enemy hideouts, U.S. forces had used the defoliant, Agent Orange. Only recently had America begun to acknowledge the devastating health effects that operation had on the native people and on their own soldiers.

Curtis said to Anne, "We could visit Times Beach. The area has memories for me."

At times Curtis wondered if he was carrying poison from Vietnam in his own system, its ill effects to emerge as he aged. (Anne, the biologist, was much more aware of the dangers.)

"We could go there on the way back to Virginia," suggested Anne.

"Okay. I say it's tentatively on the agenda. But now we'd better join the menagerie in the big house. More preparations for the official Christmas dinner."

She rose, grinning, and wiggled her behind at him. "You don't want a quickie?"

His mouth fell open, but he suspected she was teasing. Not that she wouldn't offer again. Her appetite for eroticism, it seemed to him, had expanded in the last few years.

"Uh, of course I do, but, oddly, I feel the call of duty. Rain check? Or snow check?"

"Agreed. Right now we must help the family get past this—uneasiness."

In recent years, Curtis sensed that his feeling of solidarity with siblings and cousins was stronger despite the physical distance separating them. This unexpected

142

flaring of tempers at what was in the end good news suggested more fracture lines than he'd imagined in their relationships. He'd planned to show in his dinner toast later that day that he had always valued family. Now the addition of a new member was making him question how they would all stay connected as their numbers increased. Babies not only added themselves to a family but also linked both sets of grandparents, extending and perhaps straining the reach of kin.

"You have a FACTH story ready?" he asked Anne as they entered the big house.

"I've got nothing. How about you?"

"Now that you've brought up Times Beach, I'd like to use my well-finding days there. But I'm not sure it's far enough away to count."

He was also remembering the girl he met there, but knew that wasn't a story he wanted to present to Anne, let alone the whole group. Now, like the town of Times Beach, Beth (who'd dumped him, sort of) was a ghost, at least to him.

"I suppose I could use Hawaii," Anne mused, hanging her coat on a hook by the kitchen door. "But I'm not sure what I learned there that I hadn't known already. Unless it's that I found skinny dipping in the Pacific Ocean satisfying in ways I'd never imagined!"

Chapter Twenty-two: Games

Anne had grown up near the coast in Virginia and loved spending time by the water. In his childhood, Curtis had only known Missouri creeks, rivers, and ponds; but as an adult he'd learned to appreciate the attractions (including skinny dipping) of ocean beaches. When, about ten years earlier, Anne's sister's family moved from the Norfolk area to a place on the Albemarle Sound in northeastern North Carolina, Curtis, visiting, felt the appeal of a coastal lifestyle. Now he and Anne had begun to look for a vacation/retirement home on the water.

It would not have been hard for Curtis to return to the Midwest, where he'd grown up and gone to college. He had classmates who bought property at Lake of the Ozarks. But Anne was very much a Virginian; and they'd found two good academic positions within ten miles of each other. So, neither thought of leaving the region and starting over somewhere else.

Still, beginning again, in the sense of planning a life after retirement, was becoming a subject of Curtis' daydreams. Entrepreneur (but in what venture?), travel writer (how to fund that?), stand-up comedian (but what was his shtick?). Perhaps he could become some sort of water rat.

"Serious family Scrabble tournament," announced Sam as Curtis and Anne entered the family room of the big house. "You two in?" The game had been a favorite for Curtis, Louis, and Carol growing up. This year Carol and Mark had given the twins a deluxe travel set.

"By serious, you mean multiple tables, cutthroat rules, winner-washes-no-dishes-serious?" asked Curtis. He

144

assumed there were more Scrabble sets in his brother's well-furnished house.

"Exactly. Christine, Marian, Mary Anne, and I have been playing this morning, and it occurred to us we could teach you old folks a thing or two about the game--if you're willing to put your egos on the line."

"Well, you won't get your Aunt Anne to play--she hates Scrabble--but those who aren't consumed by cooking might be ready for some old-fashioned entertainment. Hmm, it'd be interesting to see how many tables we could get going and then set up some brackets so that winners move up toward a championship round, a grand victor."

Sam agreed. "Of course, there'll also be a losers' bracket, where uncles and aunts will end up competing for grand dunce. Still, I suspect most of your generation will feel at least some comfort in being together."

Curtis, creator of the Two-Son Riddle, would play any game. Though a terrible speller, he enjoyed Scrabble, setting as a personal goal playing all seven tiles in a single turn. "Let me see if I can get my boys plus Abigail," he said. "You talk to your sisters and your folks. If Grandma joins in, that could be two more tables. Grandpa might see it as a way to stay out of the kitchen."

"There's Uncle Mark and Aunt Carol. And maybe this will draw Elizabeth out of her…state. If she and Ben are willing, we can have four tables, top two players move on to round two--two tables. A penultimate and then a final round, we'll have a winner, first, second and third runners-up. Well, and a ranking for everyone by the end of the day."

"Get the places set, request drinks and snacks, tournament begins at…shall we say 3:00?"

Suzanne, Anne, and Ben agreed to take on the cooking, and suddenly the afternoon's events were established. Of course, there is always a subtext in every game. And this time family relations were in play as well as double and triple word scores, as Curtis learned when he dared his opponents to challenge. He didn't see it coming because he was preoccupied with musings about his future.

On the drive out to Missouri, he not only wondered about the shape of his retirement (what sorts of activities or hobbies he should pursue) but also reviewed the past (how he was seen by the rest of the family). Believing he didn't conform in many ways to a Lindbloom model, he wondered how much of an outlier he truly was.

His parents, brother, and sister were technical people, skilled in calculation, quantification, consistency with rules. Although he knew he was more logical and conventional than many in his field, the rest of the family still asserted that he let emotions overrule reason.

He respected his older brother's focused college and law school career, but Curtis had deliberately chosen a liberal arts curriculum to uncover his true vocation. While he decided on English as a major fairly early, his college summers had been spent as a field researcher with the Missouri Geological Survey. It amused him now to say at cocktail parties that he had given up a promising career as a rock hound.

Unlike his sister, Curtis had never considered becoming a soldier, especially as getting deferments to pursue undergraduate and graduate degrees was commonplace at the time. Then the draft was replaced by a lottery, and he was called up almost immediately.

Still, when he finished his two years in the Army, he immediately began graduate studies in English literature

146

as if there'd been no break in his schooling. His veteran status often set him apart in the generally anti-war world of academia in the 1970s and '80st. Perhaps his liberal-leaning politics were in part an effort to downplay the fact that his brief Army career had taught him more about the importance of a social contract than he wanted to acknowledge in front of colleagues and with his fiercely independent parents and older brother.

He'd never shared much about his wartime experience with Carol, in part because whatever she did over there (in military intelligence) was top secret and what he did as a combat correspondent was for the most part routine. Now that he was wondering about exposure to Agent Orange, though, perhaps he should start a dialogue with Carol.

When Anne suggested visiting Times Beach, Curtis realized he might have had exposure to Agent Orange even before he traveled to Southeast Asia. As a well-finder twenty years ago, Curtis carried topographical maps and a barometer around the state. His job was to pinpoint precise locations for wells. Well diggers had sent core samples in to the Survey, but seldom specific topographic data. The data Curtis collected would help geologists map the state's underground.

As far as he knew, his weeks as an employee of the Geological Survey in the westernmost parts of St. Louis County had come before the use of dioxin-laden oil in the little town. But the company involved had worked in other Missouri areas; and exactly when and where contamination might have begun was uncertain.

Debate about how veterans' health and service in Vietnam was, like all aspects of that war, bitterly divisive for America. As the potential for conflict in the Middle East was escalating over the last few months, the issue of how the country cares for its veterans had heated up as well. Many feared that ruthless dictators like Saddam Hussein would use biological or chemical weapons against us if we went in to free Kuwait. So providing the proper equipment beforehand and adequate medical care afterwards meant drawing on the nation's resources.

In the middle of his first Scrabble game Curtis was surprised to see he'd played a number of words related to connections: *tie, bound, kin, joined* (the last on a triple word square for his biggest score). "Odd," he thought, and began reviewing opponents' words for clues to their subconscious worries.

Carol played "cruft," and Curtis threatened to challenge. "I can accept 'craft,' 'crust,' maybe even 'christ' as an interjection and not the deity, but 'cruft'?"

Abigail advised him, "I have a feeling this is a term in a…uh, a field you're not that familiar with. I'd think twice about challenging." She was in the lead, and Curtis couldn't tell if this potential daughter-in-law was warning him about a possible error or trying to stop him from a smart move.

Elizabeth agreed with Abigail. "You could lose your turn, and the game's close."

Curtis stared at the board, thinking not just about 'cruft' but also a possible pattern in his niece-in-law's play. She had put down some words that were almost antonyms to his own: *alone, cut, apart* (the last, interestingly, the opposite of a *part*).

"It has to be in *Webster's*," Curtis argued, pointing to the book on the nearby end table. "Not some specialized military term."

"I will get 26 points if it's legit." She looked over at the scorecard, kept by Curtis. "That puts me in a strong second place. Yeah, you might want to challenge me."

Carol was an excellent bluffer, and both Elizabeth and Abigail might be harboring some negative feelings about him as representative of his stuffy generation. But Curtis didn't want his kid sister advancing while he fell to the bottom half of the slate. He challenged and soon found himself headed into the losers' bracket with Abigail.

Chapter Twenty-three: Plows

The good news about his defeat, Curtis decided, was that he would be separated from Elizabeth in the rest of the afternoon's play. It turned out, however, that she managed to confront him from across the room in the middle of the next round. Before that happened he had an usually long exchange with Mark, who had also fallen into the bracket of losers.

Curtis didn't mind that Sam won as he'd predicted because he knew his Aunt Carol would carry away the title no matter how bad her luck in drawing tiles. She was, after all, a code breaker who saw patterns hidden from others. And she had a fiercely competitive nature that was disguised by her matter-of-fact demeanor. It would be amusing to see if the cocky younger generation could take their defeat generously.

"So," Mark asked Curtis in a break before the second round of the tournament, "let me ask something about you Southerners. "He would be at the same table with Curtis.

"You mean 'you people.' don't you?" Then Curtis realized his brother-in-law might not recognize the subtleties of Southern racism.

Mark looked quizzical. "You people? I don't follow. I'm just interested in how marriage as an institution is holding up in different parts of the country."

Curtis studied him. Surely this wasn't a hint about his relationship to Carol? Curtis admitted, "Ah, yes. Divorce rates are soaring. So, you think the conservative South will do better at clinging to traditional structures involving power?"

Again, Mark seemed not to pick up on any irony. "I just read recently that one out of every two marriages in America is now expected to end in divorce. So, is this in some areas or among certain groups? Or is it across the board?"

"Hmm," Curtis mused. "And more couples get together but don't marry, then split. So in a sense, there may be even more 'divorces' than the statistics reveal. Could it be that the California free-love model is spreading to other regions of the country."

Mark snorted. "That's not my California."

Now Curtis found himself on the other side of a cultural gap. Mark's parents had emigrated from Mexico after World War II, though nothing in his speech and little in his appearance hinted at his Hispanic origins. Carol had explained to her family that he had learned how prejudice works once he left home for college.

Curtis tried to backtrack from potential offense. "Are you thinking this might be good or bad for your cellular phone business?"

"I wasn't thinking of it in terms of business, just…how the country is changing."

"So, at least with your friends and family, marriage is still a life-time commitment?"

"It is for me," Mark said simply.

Curtis had been surprised to realize that many of the friends he'd grown up with in the Midwest were more conservative than the Southerners he associated with now. Perhaps, he reasoned, having had two races in the community for many generations, Southerners had learned how to talk about differences more openly. He had no idea what living in California was like. Professors he knew at

Stanford and Berkeley told him that not only faculty but also residents of the Bay Area\ welcomed challenges to the status quo.

"I'm hopelessly monogamous, too," said Curtis. "But a lot of social change puts pressure on traditional institutions in any situation—even family gatherings. It's amazing we can sit four tables of Scrabble without at least one big argument breaking out."

Mark grinned. "Stay tuned! And there's the big dinner coming with lots of speeches. I'm glad I'm an outlaw in-law!"

Like most in the family, he liked to pretend he was fiercely independent; but they all conformed to many traditional values—individual responsibility, patriotism, devotion to family. Mark attended PTA meetings, enrolled the family in a local YMCA, and was comfortable in Carol's Episcopal church.

Curtis thought the FACTH story taking shape in the back of his mind would be unifying rather than divisive. He said, "You know, though, that Missouri and California—the two states we grew up in—are connected by history. The famous highway from the Dust Bowl to the American Dream was Route 66. Down from Chicago through St. Louis—by the offices of Morrison, Simpson, and Lindbloom, in fact—through Fairfield, and out to L.A."

"As you know, my family came on another highway, from Guadalajara to work in the fields during the war. Later had to fight for citizenship. But that's interesting— Louis' office is on the old route?"

"Yes. You didn't know that? Well, since the highway is gone now, I guess these bits of information are fading from our cultural history. Twenty years ago we had a popular TV show based on the Mother Road, but the world moves on."

"Moves on or reconfigures itself. Four-lane interstates do what two-lane Route 66 did. The expanding cellular phone network is also like the old telephone system, which has its antecedent in the telegraph. And in the same manner, the mail service we all enjoy connects the nation. Well, the world, really."

Curtis agreed. "It's interesting, though, some people are responsible for instilling an appreciation of what we have. Take, Route 66. John Steinbeck's novel, *The Grapes of Wrath*, taught people history and a view of community. The movie with Henry Fonda re-inspired it."

"You're right about that. I tend to admire the innovators more than the publicists, the people who create something new."

Curtis was about to object to the characterization of a significant American author as a mere "publicist," but decided not to. And Mark went on. "Many of them do it less for the potential profit involved than for the benefits their work provides. You're a Missourian, do you know about the King Road Drag?"

"Some kind of car race?"

"No. Around the turn of the century, David King perfected a simple and inexpensive way to smooth rural roads as the spring thaws came. It involved two logs pulled behind a horse or mule. The first, set at an angle, broke up the big clods and pushed them toward the center of the track. The second flattened them."

"That seems like something a farmer would have figured out a long time ago."

"Well, I guess they plow fields, not lanes. Anyway, the King Road Drag had a profound effect, making it easier for people living on farms to get into town most months of the year. And, it really facilitated rural home delivery by the US Postal Service."

"Ah, another network. And cellular phones are being linked up in the same way now?"

"Yes. And not just in this country. Before long, when you're doing your research in England and Anne is back here, the two of you will be holding devices in your hand and she'll be telling you how Abigail is progressing with her first pregnancy."

"Let's say she'll be telling me about your girls winning another cross-country meet."

Curtis was pleased at this conversation, not just for the fact that they had stepped back from possible disagreement, but also because it gave him an idea for pre-retirement project. He might become what his brother-in-law termed, a "publicist."

Of course, as a scholar he already was promoting a historical phenomenon, the spread of serial publication in the nineteenth century. But perhaps he should also write about the importance of Route 66 to his generation.

That idea was taking shape in the back of his mind as he played a much better second round of Scrabble. He played "qual" down from the "e" in "vent" and, using a blank, made "bridge" plural with the play of "fasten." He was well in the lead.

His next play, "dynast," caused Marian to consider challenging. "It's not a word," Elizabeth snapped from the other table. "There's a dynasty, sure; but I've never heard 'dynast.' I say call him on it."

Marian did so and thanked her cousin-in-law for her support. Curtis wondered, though, if she was just being nice to Elizabeth, who hadn't been feeling well and seemed to feel somewhat alienated in this close family. That wouldn't surprise him, as everyone knew Marian was Mid's favorite. And losing a play at Scrabble to make someone feel better was something his mother would do.

"I realize," said Curtis, "that this would give me…uh, looks like about, oh, roughly fifty-some points; and if you remember I read a lot of old books."

Marian smiled at her uncle, and he felt she wanted to be nice to him, too.

"English teachers like to bluff, though," insisted Elizabeth. "That's what Ben's dad says."

Marian challenged; and Curtis agreed it wasn't a word.

Chapter Twenty-four: Ends

During another break, Anne asked Curtis for help with the cooking. While he knew how to and enjoyed cooking, he had assumed he would be in the way with his mother- and sister-in-law—the too many cooks rule. He wondered if something else was up.

In the kitchen, Anne took him by the arm and said, "Wait. I need my other shoes." She pulled him out toward the carriage house. He felt a biting wind and wondered if more snow were on the way.

Shoes? He was aware that she had strict rules for her biology labs: no sandals or open toes where hot or acidic spills could do damage; so same logic in a kitchen. But Anne had the comfortable walking shoes she'd recently bought in joining a church exercise program.

"You're missing all the excitement of the tournament," he told her as she pushed open the door to their room.

"I'm hoping to get my excitement right now." She turned him around toward her and pushed him back on the bed. "Remember what I promised you?" She hiked up her skirt and climbed above him on the bed.

"Now? I mean, the final round is about to . . ."

She began a kiss that threatened to permanently rearrange his lips, and her hips lowered to his hips.

This is topsy-turvy, he thought. Not only do we usually do this in the famous missionary position, I have always been the eager one, imaging sex in odds times and unexpected places.

"Can't you hurry up here?" She was fumbling with his belt, pulling on his shirt.

"I…I…"

It was a good thing he did help with his clothes because her aggressiveness led to exactly what she had promised: "a quickie."

"My goodness," he gasped as she rolled off and lay beside him. "I wasn't exactly thinking this would be part of the afternoon. Did I do something to please you?"

"No. I just felt like pleasing myself."

"Ouch!"

"Oh," she said, bussing his cheek, "I'm pleased with you, of course. It was just…just…a good time for me."

"Oh my gosh, you're not planning on another child are you? You told me you had your tubes tied after Mary Anne."

"No, silly. It's our children who are going to have the babies from now on. Ben and Elizabeth are just the first parents-to-be of their generation."

"So the news got you in the mood? Well, I'm not complaining."

"I was pretty sure you wouldn't."

He sat up and began buttoning his shirt. "So, though we aren't getting ready to be parents a fourth time, we do have to prepare to be grandparents a first time. That confirms my notion that we are in a pre-retirement phase, initiating projects that we will pursue into our senior years."

"That's okay for you, but remember I took some time out of my career when the kids were little, so I'm thinking more about having my most productive professional years in the next decade or so. You go…um…you go take up skydiving or something."

"You know, I did have an idea about what to do. Mark and I were talking about Route 66 earlier. California and Missouri are linked by that road and by its significance."

"The two of you could buy an old truck and rattle along from here to there, recalling the good old days."

Very much a Virginian, she had never been drawn to the culture of the West or the Midwest, comparing places like Dodge City negatively to Williamsburg, seeing the St. Louis Arch as insignificant against the wonders of Monticello."

"No, but I might write a book about The Mother Road."

"It's not been done," she teased, "by…oh, I don't know, by John Steinbeck?"

"Of course there's *The Grapes of Wrath*, but that's the past. Maybe we need a book about the future after Route 66. You know, the road's been decommissioned, superseded by interstates. I'm not sure everyone's happy with that, the loss of a key symbol of American history."

"Hmm. You have a point there. Not just the road itself, but what came with it: the overdone neon motel signs, the greasy roadside diners, the not-really-your-mom-and-pop souvenir places."

"Those things do have an odd charm; they're camp. But we need to reconfigure them for the future. We need to take the best from the past and bring it into the future."

"Why don't you focus on the butt-trays?"

158

"The what?"

"I've seen them at your favorite highway knick-knack stores: the model of a toilet that's an ashtray. The ashes go in the can, so to speak, and you can rest your cigarette where the seat's split in the front."

"Ah, a butt dump. Yes, that's attractive and brings back wonderful memories. I could even specialize on the hillbilly version: an outhouse three-holer."

"Now you're talking, but let's get our asses back where they're supposed to be." She gave his a solid swat. "And don't look too guilty or too happy."

"I'll try." He winked. "And I assume you don't really need to change your shoes?"

Back in the Scrabble tournament he fought the urge to smile when he thought about what had happened not many minutes earlier and how unlikely it was those at his table would guess. What they had done—plus the conversation they'd had about butt-trays—also made him chuckle to himself when he thought about an episode from his youth.

The term he used for one of those ashtrays, a "butt dump," took his mind back to Beth, a girl he would ironically brag to his college friends he had "dumped" one summer night when he worked for the state geological survey as a well finder.

Beth was a waitress in the Eureka diner where Curtis ate at the end of his workdays for several weeks. She lived three miles away in Times Beach, where dioxin had been "dumped" to settle road dust. A little older than Curtis, she enjoyed teasing the "college boy."

"So, whenever you look for a well, you ask about the farmer's daughter?" she asked one time.

"The daughter? No…I'm just there to locate…to see the place that…"

"But you like someone to hold your hand as you go into the bushes, don't you?" She put her hand on his hand as he was bringing a forkful of mashed potatoes up to his mouth. "You probably want to put your hand right on the…the right place."

She'd let go of his hand, reached up to brush an invisible speck off the breast that swelled her blouse, and let her hand linger there.

Beth had told Curtis she had no desire to go to college or to rise in a profession. She was just waiting for the right guy to come into her life, make her a wife and a mother, give her a little house with a yard and nice neighbors.

"You're not that guy, college boy, but I do kind of like you."

Curtis would feel her hip bump against his hip as she went around the counter to wait on one of the booths, would find her shoulder brushing his back as she returned, would see her look back at him and wink as she bent over to arrange supplies in a cabinet.

She told him one night he should come back when her shift was ending, at 1:00 in the morning. She could give him a free piece of pie. "You like cherry, don't she you?" she'd grin. "You know…sweet cherry pie."

So he did come by late the last night he would work the area. As she came out, she saw him standing by his car at the end of the parking lot. "Over here." she whispered and waved at the end of the diner.

Around the back by the trash bins she let him get immediately to second base. Then she lay down beside the bins. "Dump me," she said. "Dump me, college boy." How sweet she had been!

Whatever happened to Diner Beth, he wondered? They'd both grown up on fabled Route 66. She lived in a town destroyed by poison while he was nurtured by a close, prosperous community. Had she left Times Beach, or did she stay and get sick? Did history dump her as it carried him forward to a successful and fulfilling life? Did location determine destiny?

Studying the Scrabble board for a place to play the Z, he was reminded of how fortunate his life had been.

Chapter Twenty-five: Fields

Curtis would begin his FACTH by asserting, "Cocker spaniels have no street sense." And then he'd explain that that was why at their home in Virginia "we have a high, solid fence around the back yard. They've never learned much about the outside world."

Anne, guessing where the story was going, might add, "He often takes the sisters, twins from the same litter, with him to my parents' little cottage in North Carolina. He has to keep their leashes on them at all times." Curtis would go down there to take care of minor maintenance problems: replacing a torn screen, filling a hole behind the bulkhead, shampooing the carpet.

Sam was likely to interject, "I've read about cockers. While they can find birds by their scent, they have no idea where they've been or where they are in relationship to a starting point."

So Curtis would continue. "The Carters, Anne's parents, have this little beach house, as you know, near Edenton, northeast corner of the state. That village isn't even as big as Rural." The Virginia town they lived in might be all of five thousand, not counting college students.

"Dullsville, II," he imagined one of the nieces from St. Louis or Berkeley observing.

"At least there's the Albemarle Sound," explained Anne, "always a source of entertainment for kids." Anne's sister and family lived next door in a year-round home.

Picking up on her lead, Curtis would say, "Princess and the Queen must have thought they deserved entertainment, too. When they escaped that one time from the Dodge Colt, they were ready to chase other dogs, stray cats, field mice."

"How did they get away from you?" someone would ask, and he would have to explain.

"The back seats go down flat, expanding the cargo area, and there's a gate between them and me. They usually sleep, but this time, Queen--the Alpha dog, as you might guess from her name--was restless. Maybe she smelled the cookies I had stashed away. Anyway, she pawed the gate in some way, and it fell back on top of both dogs."

"And they were in the front seat with you in a flash," laughed Ethel, the animal lover. "Just the way Dorothy would be...if she couldn't find a way out of the car altogether."

"You're right. She's ready to eat even if I'm trucking down a two-lane road at 55 miles per hour. So, I have to get the gate back up; and that means a stop. This is flatland, fields all around me. I spot a farm road--really, two tractor tire tracks in the dirt--and pull off."

Curtis knew that the personal experience of the Midwesterners and Westerners could produce no picture of a soy bean field in late fall: the plants about eighteen inches tall, dark green leaves, parallel rows down the rich, sandy, delta soil. Nor would any but Carol be able to envision the rice paddies, the water buffalo, the twin buckets carried across the shoulders that Curtis remembered from another flatland--the Mekong Delta of Vietnam. That's what he had passed on that day he wandered away from a base, a moment of madness on a day he would not mention in his FACTH, despite its relevance.

"As you'll see in a moment, I could have been killed if human nature--well, if canine nature—hadn't asserted itself. I had pulled into a soybean field. Pointing a stern finger at 'Royalty'--their collective name—I said, 'stay,' and backed out of the driver's side door."

Again, Ethel was quick to pick up. "They got past you."

"Call of the wild," suggested Sam, looking at the window as if he'd planned, like Dorothy, to follow some primitive instinct out into the winter snow.

"Queen was on the ground. Princess followed, but I caught her. A sweet dog, she'll let me do anything to her. So, I pitched her back in and looked for Queen."

"Not in the road, I hope?"

"On the shoulder, but, fortunately, nose to the ground. And bless the Lord, there were no cars coming either way!" He paused, then lowered his voice conspiratorially. "If she'd been in the road, and a car coming, I knew I might as well lie down there with her. Queen is Anne's dog. If she were run over, I would have said, 'Take me, too, Lord. Take me now.'"

Anne would open her eyes wide in mock objection to this depiction of her.

"So, when Queen stopped…to do what dogs do, to leave her mark, so to speak…I pounced on her." He paused, anticipating chuckles. "I was polite, though, and let her finish."

Sam continued the story, "Then you turned and were face-to-face with a wolf."

"No wolves," said Curtis. "But the danger wasn't over. I got her back to the car, plunked her down on the front seat so I could fix the gate."

164

"She didn't get away again?" asked Ethel.

"She did! Sly fox, right between my legs. But this time she went away from the road, out into the field. So again, I kept Princess in the car and went after her. She'd gone about ten yards or so down the path, then turned into the soy beans."

Anne added. "If you've never seen them, it's a pretty sight in the fall. The fields are completely flat, so the rows are straight and go as far as a mile sometimes."

"That's right," agreed Curtis. "Queen was prancing down between two rows, her cocker spaniel ears flopping, her nose up to smell the air. All I could do was play defense, like a basketball player: stay between the other player and the goal behind me."

"The goal being the road in this case," Ethel pointed out.

"Yes. I just had to keep her from getting past me and flattened by a speeding car. But then, as I said earlier, canine nature kicked in. Or something pretty deep inside her." He paused. "Now, I know we can't read a dog's mind. Shoot, we can't even put their thoughts into our words, but still, that day I felt I knew what Queen was thinking."

"Oh?"

"You see, all of a sudden, Queen stopped where she was and looked around--ahead, to this side, to that. She had to stretch her neck to see over the soybean plants, they were that tall. She was the picture of alertness, scouting the territory before making a dash for wherever."

Curtis' moment of wanting to be free when he'd been a reporter in Vietnam came back with a rush. He had to get past this moment in the dog story.

"Queen was free, the world completely open around her; she could escape all barriers. But then she froze. And I am honestly convinced she thought something like, 'I have never in my life seen anything that remotely resembles this. Where the heck am I? There are no sidewalks here, no front lawns, not a house in sight. This is an alien landscape, a foreign world.'"

Ethel agreed. "I can understand that--a town dog out in the country."

Curtis remembered passing through the fence of the base near Can Tho, walking past rice fields, wandering into a clump of banana trees. The branches arched over the path, blocking the sun, and he found himself standing in what was almost a tunnel or a cave. He became aware of flitting shadows, unpleasant smells, strange animal (and human?) sounds. The insane impulse to dessert, to find the river, to escape by boat, evaporated.

It occurred to Curtis that such places he'd traveled to in Vietnam could well have been saturated with Agent Orange. For all he knew, his blood was full of dioxin.

He went on. "And I tell you, she looked around, then she looked back at me. I am certain she thinks: 'Hmm, I know that guy, that guy yelling at me to get back here. He keeps me on a leash and makes me walk in the yard and takes me to the vet, but…but, you know, he also gives me food and belly rubs. I understand him. Out here,' she says to herself, again looking around, 'it's weird. I don't know how this place works. And I don't trust it.'"

"You mean that she came back to you on her own?" Ethel smiled.

"Exactly. She took one last glance around, turned, and trotted back down the row to the double tire tracks (where I'd moved, too, in a parallel fashion, still playing defense), came right up to me, and let me swoop her up, plunk her back in the car."

Anne added. "Where Princess was happy to see her. They're never apart."

Sam said, "Well, I say she bailed. Took the easy way out. So many of us do that, I guess." Curtis was pretty sure he didn't see himself as one who missed opportunities to rebel.

"If there're ever," he concluded, "happy endings to shaggy dog stories, this has to be one of them."

On the morning of his stroll in Vietnam, Curtis had watched four soldiers bag what they could of two men blown to pieces when a rocket landed in their bunker. Choppered in the day before to interview members of an intelligence unit, he'd drunk beer with Duke and Roy while waiting for a ride out. They had gone on perimeter guard duty, and he sacked out in their hootch. The shells came with the first light of dawn.

Curtis, standing in a clump of banana trees, later understood at an almost visceral level something so important that he had struggled ever since for ways and places to communicate it. Far away, close to home.

Part 6: Anne

Chapter Twenty-six: Genes

"Are you coming in to lick your wounds?" Anne teased Curtis when he sought her out in the kitchen at the end of the Scrabble tournament.

"My wounds are old ones; you'd better see to these two younger men."

His son and nephew were, they said, "resorting to drink." Each was opening a Coke. Sam (third place) said, "You might have warned us, Uncle Curtis."

Justin agreed. "Something came over Aunt Carol, a strange look in her eye and she didn't hear anything we said." Elizabeth had been a respectable second place.

"You saw her game face," laughed Curtis. "I grew up with it."

Suzanne said, "Louis knows about it, too. Isn't that right, Mother?"

"She's my youngest child but not the least fearsome," laughed Mid.

Anne told the boys, "Listen, you had your triumph with the technology of 'Route 66 to Palestine.' And you should have known the women would prove superior in…well, in everything else."

Justin challenged her. "And why is that?"

She decided not to say "Balls" as an answer, but the thought was there. Instead she said, "For one thing, you're all descendants of a single woman--not 'chips off the old block,' but recipients of Eve's mtDNA. Of course, in your line it's thinned down quite a bit."

"Come again?" asked Sam.

Curtis laughed. "Ah, I've heard this story more than once. Take your drinks over to the breakfast nook, and you'll learn something about who you are, about who we all are."

Anne sat with them at the little table with a view of the brick patio, the gymnasium, and the carriage house. "Modern genetics has found that we are all descendants of a single woman who lived in Africa probably about 100,000-200,000 years ago."

"You mean, an Adam and an Eve, though, don't you?" asked Justin. He tried to avoid showing interest in his parents' fields, English and biology, especially to his male peers.

"Nope. Mitochondrial DNA--we can shorten that to mtDNA--is passed from mother to offspring without recombination; so all mtDNA in every living person--that is, all anatomically modern humans--is directly descended from a single woman. We all have her DNA."

"But male DNA?" asked Sam.

"Sorry. Their mtDNA is slated for destruction in the embryo, so, when we trace our ancestors back, it's through the maternal line, back to what we think of as the one common mother of us all."

"Huh," said Justin.

Suzanne, listening from the stove (where she was checking on the ham), said, "So, no wonder you couldn't beat your aunt. She's inherited all the good stuff, whereas you guys have--oh, I don't know--I guess, you have a kind of watered down version of what makes us human."

"I think we've heard enough of this feminist science," huffed Sam. "Let's go back to some manly activities like table tennis."

Anne was about to remind them that their cousins Christie and Marian were improving at a rapid rate and might end the weekend as champions there, too. But she decided too much talk about any battle of the sexes was inappropriate for the family gathering, though she had been thinking a lot about them herself recently.

She did not like to admit that her life had been restricted because she was a woman. And now, as new and greater opportunities were coming to her almost faster than she could take advantage of them, she generally sidestepped questions about the discrimination she had faced.

She had chosen to work part time for more than a decade so she could be home with her children and to give Curtis support for his career. At times she felt, after getting her Ph.D., that she'd suffered arrested development in her professional life.

But now, as Curtis was pulling back, looking for new challenges outside of his profession, Anne was becoming more and more excited about teaching and about a new research project she'd begun centered on the ecology of outcrops. She felt she was entering a period of delayed gratification in terms of her professional life.

Of course, here she was in the kitchen with Mid and Suzanne while her husband was playing games and talking sports with his nephews. A division of labor and of interests remained with the sexes. Though both men and women were participants in the FACTH competition, for example, more women were reluctant and more men eager to be the center of attention.

She recalled how she'd been advised in graduate school about speaking in front of groups. "Do not smile," her (male) mentor (there were no female professors at the time) had told her when she gave her first major lecture in the department. "And stay behind the podium. You don't want your audience to be distracted by your legs, as lovely as they are."

Dr. Watson, her major professor, was grandfatherly in his dealing with her, confident that he was protecting her from the competitive arena where men inevitably dominated. But as her generation brought more women into the professions, the model of the workplace expanded.

At this Christmas celebration she was reminded that Curtis' mother and his sister had advanced the cause of women. The former, a nurse in WWII, and the latter, an Army officer and computer expert, were good examples of working women. It had taken some years for Anne, the Southerner, to value their directness and their willingness to take public stances.

The image of Mitochondrial Eve came back, the mother of us all. Eve's descendants were now so numerous and spread so far around the globe that they seemed less able--or less willing--to recognize a common origin. Divisions between individuals and among groups dominated the world's mindset. According to Carol, we're on the brink of a war that will echo religious divides from the era of crusades. And Americans were lining up on different sides of the issue.

Anne had to acknowledge splits threatening the fragile harmony in this reunion event. Cousins from different parts of the country reflected their regional cultures. And even the first generation of siblings, who had grown up together in a small town along Route 66, were held together less strongly by the bonds of their youth.

This was not much the case in her own family, at least for now. Anne's one sister, husband, and children

172

lived about three hours from Rural; her parents were even closer. So the Carters saw each other frequently and shared the South--well, the New South's--views. But her own children? Would Justin, Carol, and Mary Anne drift apart as each left home? Would it be possible for Curtis and her to host a family reunion for them in twenty-five years, especially when they would have, like Ben, added another generation to the fold?

As if called up by these musings, Carol, former Army code-breaker and now successful high tech entrepreneur, came into the kitchen. "Anne," she asked, "could I borrow you for a minute? A few questions about the order of events."

Though it seemed odd that she would need a private meeting for such a simple matter, Anne agreed and followed her down the hall to the living room. "I don't think we have to follow a strict timetable," she said. And then added with a laugh, "Or that we'd be able to."

Carol sat in one of the armchairs and gestured to another. "I know. It's something else."

She glanced back to see that they were alone. "Do you think Grandpa's okay?"

"Okay? Well, yes, I guess. I mean did you see…did he do something odd?"

Anne was never prepared for her sister-in-law's abrupt manner. There was no small talk leading to an important question or casual observation that introduced a topic she had been mulling over. Instead she went directly to the matter at hand.

"He remembers less of what happened yesterday and talks more about his childhood. He went on for an hour with Mark about two Swedish cousins he used to play with in a band--even sang some of the lyrics of their old tunes--but couldn't seem to call up our daughters' names."

"I haven't noticed, but, then again, I've not been with him much. He's been off in his room, reading, I assumed. Have you talked to anyone else?"

"I'm going to to speak with Louis, but, since he sees Dad more frequently, he may not notice slow change. It's been over a year since we visited, so differences are more noticeable."

"What about Grandmother?"

Carol shrugged. "She'd never tell. And I suspect she's covering for any lapses."

"How…how bad do you think it is?'

Carol shrugged. "Bad enough that you'd better see what you think."

After they were back in the kitchen, Anne wondered why Carol had come to her, the in-law, rather than to her brother Curtis.

Chapter Twenty-seven: Tastes

Anne knew if Mid had suspicions about Grandpa's mental capacity, she would keep them to herself. And their son Curtis would not let himself see such signs in a father he admired. So, rather than talk to her husband, she decided to have a talk with her father-in-law herself.

As most of the family were off doing whatever they needed to be ready for the big dinner, Anne knocked on the frame of the open door to the downstairs guest room. Oscar, looking up from a book he was reading, waved at the matching easy chair by the fireplace. "Come in, sit. By the fire feels good. I think we're going to get another storm."

"I hope not for those of us who have to travel. But I was going to ask for help with my FACTH. I don't think everyone wants to sit for biology lessons." She had also become worried that a male-female rivalry was brewing in this storytelling completion, a skirmish in the battle-of-the-sexes. But she wouldn't tell her father-in-law that.

"Grandmother has advised me against physics lectures, too, so I guess we academics are going to have fall back on personal stories." He took a book of matches from a little table beside him and relit his pipe. Suzanne would only allow him to smoke in this one room. Like everyone else in the family, she'd tried to get him to quit altogether.

Anne said, "I'm not particularly fond of talking about myself."

"Mid says I'm spend too much time doing that these days, reliving my youth. I'm supposed to get out more, go to movies, read new books."

"Curtis tells me there are some good writers now—Toni Morrison, Salmon Rushdie, others I can't think of right now."

"I still prefer Jack London, Hemingway. And for a bit of escape, something like *The Phantom of the Opera*." He held up the book he'd been reading.

"I guess I've only seen the movie version."

"There, too, the old days win out. We had the stars—Lon Chaney and Mary Philbin, Garbo, Gable, Bogart and Bacall. And you can watch their films on television in the comfort of your living room. No reason to go to a theater where—the…the, uh, youngsters are noisy, undisciplined. We're happy to stay home."

She knew that wasn't completely true for Mid. "Well, with two 'youngsters' still in the house, Curtis and I try to keep up a bit with current trends." She paused. "Actually, I was going to get your opinion on something else. Curtis is thinking of writing about the future of Route 66. What do you think?"

"The future? Route 66 belongs the past." He sighed. "It's part of so many things that are fading while ridiculous fads take their places. Take the music today; it's horrible. That Madonna!"

Anne could see he was not unhappy to talk on the subject of contemporary tastes. "She's very popular, though," she offered.

"Ah, it's all the electronic amplification. If you took away the microphones and other gimmicks, you could tell in a second that she's no Rosemary Clooney or Ella Fitzgerald."

"The young people do seem to like her, even my daughter."

176

"They like the glitter and her revealing outfits. It's all prancing and…" He was having trouble finding the right words, especially in front of his daughter-in-law. "Listen, Hollywood can make anyone famous these days."

"I see. With the right equipment, we can all be stars. Maybe it's good that the pool of talent has expanded exponentially."

"No, the real talent gets lost in the crowd. Not like it was in my day. With the Big Bands, singers had to be musicians, work with the orchestra, know their cues. It's Madonna's back-up crew that keep the performance together."

Anne watched him draw deeply on his pipe and exhale a cloud of smoke up toward his reading light. She asked, "You still play with your group, The Rockers of Age."

"Yes, though some of my fellow musicians are afraid we're falling behind the times, that we need to change our style."

"I can see some sense in that. You don't want your audience to dwindle down to…to a single group." She had been about to say "a tiny group of old-timers."

"Well, it's…it's not easy to change what you've been doing for years." He emptied the contents of his pipe into the ashtray. "I've got a fine collection of records from the old days. They're still my models. And I don't need any new sound system to play them, either."

Listening to her father-in-law looking backward, Anne couldn't help looking forward into her own future, to what this man's son might be like as he aged. She knew that her social life had been restricted by Curtis, who by nature (or because of the nature of his family) had always been a bit of a loner.

Was his new talk about exciting pre-retirement projects truthful? Or was he fantasizing about activities that would never materialize in real life? Would he buy a second house on the water, take up hobbies like sailing, move away from scholarship to write for a popular audience? If so, her own future would be brighter.

On the other hand, he might be proposing his "pre-retirement" approach to the next few years as a way of deliberately avoiding the future: all talk and no action. She hoped not, though that might allow her to blossom as a "pre-mid-life" active woman (if such a category existed).

She thought about the proposed stop at Times Beach on their way back to Virginia. For her it was a biological field trip that looked toward to the coming spring semester. But Curtis seemed interested for reasons that pointed back to his past. He was connecting Route 66, the road through Times Beach, with his growing up.

A few years ago he had come back from the 25th reunion of his high school class full of stories he now looked for opportunities to tell. And the weekend event (she had not been able to attend) had led to semi-regular correspondence with friends from his youth. Was he looking back to understand the present and prepare for the future; or was he, a scholar of nineteenth century literature—and thus a professional student of history— retreating further into the past?

Curtis had also been thoughtful about dioxin poison in the little village of Times Beach. She'd quizzed him earlier about his exposure to Agent Orange in Vietnam, but he'd always brushed off her concerns. Now he seemed to be thinking more about that part of his personal history.

She knew veterans of World War II who, in retirement, wanted to return to the places they'd served, to Normandy or Italy. One of her uncles, a former Marine

178

who'd fought in the Pacific, was considering writing a book about training dogs for combat and their performance in battle. She felt Curtis had stories to tell about his service, though he'd never shared much with her. All she had were a number of phrases that meant something to his few Army buddies: "No sweat, GI"; "Dee-dee-mow"; "Same-same."

She remembered a recent moment with a colleague in the chemistry department, a Korean war vet, who, at a retirement party in his honor, talked quietly with her about his R & R in Japan. "We called it 'I and I'—'Intercourse and Intoxication'—or 'A & A'—'Alcohol and'—excuse me—'Ass'. But it's one of those experiences that stays with you longer than you think at the time."

"Oh?" she had asked innocently.

"You see, there were streets in Tokyo where women, young women, would just be…oh, standing around. They were not, um, hustling exactly, but they'd let us buy them drinks and talk. It's odd: they seemed to be sympathetic to our stories."

"Their fathers and uncles and brothers had had their war, I guess."

"Yes. But, you know, the American women there, the wives of military or businessmen, had had relatives in the last war. But they didn't want us bothering them. It was if we'd made some mistake ending up in conflict. And, if we did, why were we bothering them with our worries? But the Japanese girls, now, all shy and giggly, they'd listen to us for hours on end. They'd say, 'You, chosen, go?' which meant they were sad we had to return to such a terrible ordeal."

"Did you tell your stories when you got home? Were there women who wanted to hear?"

He sighed. "No. We put it all behind us. Or at least, as we best we could. Maybe now, when I have the leisure, I'll start putting some of those memories down on paper. Somebody could learn something from them about what war does to young men."

As the family was getting before-dinner drinks and snacks, she asked Curtis nervously, "What's your FACTH story going to be about?"

Chapter Twenty-eight: Balls

When Curtis told her he would talk about a soybean field for his FACTH story, Anne relaxed. She knew what he would recall: a time, not too recent, when their cocker spaniels, Queen and Princess, got away from him in a field down in North Carolina. His speech, then, would not show a fixation with the past or pit men against women in response to current debate. Her sense of comfort didn't last long, however.

"They let anyone into college these days," she heard Oscar tell Justin and Sam as they were arranging serving dishes and place settings in the dining room. "Colleges have no standards. You boys are bright, and you might do better to go directly into the workplace."

Anne was about to raise objections not just to this view, but also to his suggesting this to a young man already in college and one in the process of applying. But Carol more quickly supported her father. "The military is doing the same thing. It's harder and harder to get qualified personnel, so they're lowering the levels on aptitude tests, waiving previous restrictions about criminal records, offering big bonuses."

Louis and Suzanne's table with extra leafs could sit sixteen. For this occasion they'd arranged a drop-leaf table, nearly as large, from the main hallway. Anne knew they often hosted dinner parties for more than were in the house now.

"Just a minute," she said to Carol. "I've read studies that show the all-volunteer military is better educated than its predecessor." Turning to the boys, she added, "And I know something myself about college standards for admission. Studies show they're not falling."

Carol huffed. "There are studies to prove anything in education. And I'm telling you what my friends in the military say is based upon their firsthand experience."

Grandpa was eager to add, "Nowadays we hire consultants to do research; and they know that they get paid to produce what's wanted by the people who hire them. We've had an explosion of unqualified, so-called 'experts'—who can't hold a regular job themselves. They generate pages and pages of meaningless garbage and call it 'data.'"

Anne watched her son and his cousin look with interest at each person who spoke. But she suspected they were primarily being polite and would be alert for an early opportunity to escape this grown-up discussion.

"You're making assumptions that, because more people go to college, the additional numbers come from under-qualified individuals. But what's happening is that more people whose parents didn't have the opportunity or the resources to attend in the past now have the chance to send their children because the country's more prosperous."

Sam added. "My guidance counselor says that each year more students take the SAT's and more apply to college."

Oscar scoffed. "Accepting more students just means more money for the colleges. They're filling up dormitories and classrooms with whoever they can find."

Carol agreed. "Army recruiters have to reach their quotas. The qualifications are adjusted to generate the necessary troop numbers."

"And we're getting too many international students," insisted Oscar. "Many of them can't speak English, but they swell the size of the institution."

Anne decided not to point out that Oscar had been retired for a decade and that, according to Mid, paid little attention to what was going on at his former institution. Even if what he claimed was partly accurate, he was too eager to take a negative view. But she realized this was a conversation that had gained a head of steam, and she didn't think she'd been able to bring it to a stop by herself.

She thought about her family's dinner table in the house where she'd grown up. Her father had had a friend build it from heavy pine boards. They had a captain's chair at each end and two benches on the sides where two (three if children) could sit. But when she or her sister had friends over, they spilled over into living room using card tables, some balancing dishes on their laps. Those were loosely organized but enjoyable events.

Her own dining room in Virginia was slightly bigger than her parents', but she and Curtis couldn't comfortably sit more than eight. She began to think about her children, their future partners, possible grandchildren. Where would they all fit, especially if there were friction between certain family members? Should they look for a bigger house at the time their children were moving out? How big would the houses of her grandchildren have to be?

Her mind ran through lectures she gave in her introductory biology course about crowding. She knew how a foreign element can appear in an organism, take over that host, but ultimately destroy the very world it had colonized. Invasive plants can spread quickly and grow so densely that native species are crowded out. Introduced plants can also fill or redirect waterways. The fundamental nature of an ecosystem is disrupted by restrictions in space and resources. Is it the same with people?

Anne often used such instances of crowding in order to get the students' attention about ecological principles. But she also utilized a health risk too often ignored by young people—especially by men, who so often possess an illogical faith in their own invulnerability.

"Testicles," would be her first word that day. Men and women would look up, and she would click on the projector. Overhead diagrams—a drawing showing the location of organs, a cross section of a healthy testes, the photograph of an ugly tumor—would appear over her shoulder. "It's a prime location for trouble. I don't just mean that some men are guided by these organs more than their brains, though that can happen. What I'm talking about is a condition too often not recognized as serious—a hard, painless lump in the testicle."

Pretending not to see any wincing, she would remind the women that they should be as aware of what she was going to say as their male classmates. "They can be the site of a particularly deadly form of cancer for your boyfriend, your brother, one day your husband."

Some of the women, who had been suppressing grins and glancing left and right at the men, would drop their eyes.

"It can start right here," Anne said, pointing at the screen, "and take over other organs via lymphatic pathways: lung, liver, brain, bone, kidney, adrenal gland and spleen in that order. That's why you…," she pointed at specific male students, "…and you and you should be regularly examining your testicles."

There would be a few more chuckles at this point, some embarrassed looking down at the floor, an awkward

184

shifting in seats. To relieve some of the pressure she showed a chart.

"It's the most common cancer affecting men between the ages of 15 and 35. Here's how it happens. Some of our genes control when our cells grow, divide into new cells, and die. Others slow down division or make cells die at the right time. If the tumor suppressors don't function correctly, cancerous cells, which can double in number in as little as ten days, can be produced. "

She brought up a slide of the circulatory system.

"Another thing the cancer cell genes are able to do is redirect blood flow, cutting off healthy cells and feeding themselves. That's when the tumor begins to grow. And it's when cancer cells can travel through the circulatory system to the rest of the body."

She had given talks like this enough times to know she would lose her audience's attention if she went on too long with the details of disease and destruction.

"Unlike a parasite, which finds a way to coexist with a host or to propagate to another organism, the cancer in the end destroys its own home. Cancer cells kill the normal cells; and then the body of all cells finally passes away. But the delicate balance of an organism—or a group of organisms—can be disrupted with few initial signs of trouble. That's one of the reasons you're in this class: to learn about biological systems, their support and preservation."

Rather than slip away from the debate about lowering standards, as Anne had expected, Sam and Justin became more involved. Each had stories about classes in which it was impossible to fail, and both Grandpa and Aunt Carol insisted that had never been the case in the past.

"This is what's happening to our country," insisted Oscar. "When the next big crisis comes, we're not going to have the intelligence to see it or the backbone to withstand it."

Carol nodded. "The Middle East is not the only tinder box in this world. I'm very worried about what rogue dictators like Saddam Hussein will do. But we've got China to worry about now that the Soviet Union is crumbling. A reunited Germany?—I don't know what to think about that. It's certainly no time to relax and assume we can coast on our past achievements."

Anne worried less about outside threats and more about internal attitudes. Would fear of the future and the division of people into opposing camps generate a mentality that destroyed them all? Would a crippling lack of faith start in families like this one and spread?

Chapter Twenty-nine: Landscapes

"Mark, can I ask you a question?" Anne had sought him out in the gymnasium where he was encouraging his daughters to finish their workouts and get ready for dinner.

"Sure, so long as it's not which fork to use for the salad or if I can fold cloth napkins into swans." He'd been sitting on one of the weight lifting benches and now slid over to make room for her. He was watching the trees bend to the wind on the other side of the picture window.

She laughed. "No, this is…well, it's about family. Carol asked me if I thought Dad was…doing okay these days."

She waved at her nieces as one left the treadmill, the other an exercise bicycle, and headed off to shower in the cottage. "Cover up out there," she cautioned. "It's cold."

Mark looked more serious. "Yes, she's mentioned some worry. I'm not the best judge, though, as I don't go as far back as you guys. Well, and there is a culture gap."

"It's not really that." She bit her lower lip, puzzling. "It's why Carol spoke to me, not Curtis. And I think she'll talk with Suzanne. We're sort of bypassing the men, it seems to me."

"Carol seldom bypasses anyone or anything. Her approach is head-on and to the point. Sometimes that's not the most pleasant way to go, but it's who she is."

"I've known that for some time. In fact, I've learned that there are times when bluntness is much better than Southern politeness…or the California sunshine way."

He laughed. "Yes, blind optimism doesn't always play well. My traditions can be jarring, too, out there. Maybe because we learn about hardships early and see how difficult it is to endure. I lost both my parents when young. Well, you know something about loss also." Anne's father had passed away the previous year. After numerous childhood bouts with pneumonia, he'd had respiratory troubles throughout most of his adulthood. Lung surgery left him unable to continue in his highway department job; and later he suffered from hepatitis, possibly contracted from blood transfusions during the operation.

"Yes," agreed Anne. "Landscape shapes your view more than we realize when we're young. I've lived most of my life in the South, where the summers are lush and the winters are not harsh. I tend to look on the bright side of things. I was unsettled by the deserts we saw when we met you and Carol in Nevada. So stark and bleak."

Curtis had been attending a conference in Reno, and Mark and Carol drove up with the twins, then four years old. Anne's mother had stayed with her children back in Virginia.

Mark smiled. "It all looked pretty familiar to me." He'd grown up on a remote farm in the Mexican state of Chihuahua another high desert, if a warmer one.

She asked, "Remember driving out to Silver City?"

"A ghost town haunted by gold seekers of the past. Didn't we go over to Virginia City, too?"

"Yeah. Silly me, thinking because it had 'Virginia' in its name, the area wouldn't as grim as what we'd seen around Silver City. And that place wasn't 'glittery' either." A particular picture from that experience flashed through her mind.

"Fairfield is as green as Virginia," said Mark, "even if the trees are stunted. That's not from climate, though, but over-harvesting and not replenishing the soil."

"Well, it's familiar and comforting to Oscar, though I think Mid would like to travel more, see other places." She frowned. "I wonder if he truly appreciates the land and the climate or is he just retreating, protecting himself from change. His focus is more on the past than the future, one of the signs of…of aging." She didn't want to use a harsher word.

"You think he should want to move to Virginia? Milder weather, easier life?"

"No, not that. He wouldn't like our busy life—church, entertaining, politics. He's a stay-at-home, quiet life guy."

"You're asking the wrong man, then, even if the other guys—Curtis and Louis—don't want to psychoanalyze their father." In other words, Mark wasn't going to assert that his father-in-law was becoming senile.

On her way back to the house, Anne found herself thinking about desolate lands, the lost hopes of gold seekers, the disease of greed, and, in the end, of cancer …and not as a metaphor.

She, Curtis, Mark, and Carol had gone to the Virginia City newspaper office where Mark Twain might be said to have begun his writing career. The four tourists stepped out of their rental car in a city parking lot that ended at a steep drop off to a treeless desert below and looked out to mountains perhaps twenty miles beyond. They were standing on the edge of a vast empty space.

Though a biologist who understood how many forms of life inhabited even that landscape, Anne felt such conditions would not have appeared hospitable to early settlers. There were unseen dangers out there then and now.

"Watch that last step," Curtis had joked. "It's a lulu."

"Let's take a picture," Mark laughed. "You know, just back up a lit-tle bit-ty bit."

Anne had a cousin, a geologist, who'd lived in Nevada for more than a decade. Hired by mining companies to explore remote areas for possible sources of gold, he's been diagnosed recently with thyroid cancer. Uranium deposits in the isolated regions he camped in for months at a time might have been a factor, though his employers naturally denied the possibility. But recent events had raised other worries about exposure to radiation in the Silver State.

Studies of atomic bomb testing in the 1950s were confirming the deadly consequences for those exposed to fallout. And in 1987 Congress authorized an underground storage facility for spent nuclear fuel in Nevada. Power plants from all over the country would be shipping radioactive waste to be buried deep under the mountains, despite the protests of conservationists and many residents.

While the state's low population and its desert terrain made it preferable to other regions of the country for spent uranium storage (reasons it was chosen for testing earlier), there was still a feeling that whatever plant and animal life maintained a livelihood there would be sitting on known and unknown causes of disease, just as residents of Times Beach, Missouri, had been.

Was it too much of a leap to think that, in the Lindbloom family past, forces had been at work for years that could undermine the clan's structure? The oldest members would be affected by time, of course, gradually losing ability and authority as their children matured and the world they'd known evolved into new forms. Resisting change could weaken the family. Too, decisions they'd made years ago might have produced fissures in relationships only becoming visible now.

Children might follow their parents' example and adopt their values, but never totally. The challenges each generation faces, although often analogous to those confronted by their predecessors, are still distinctive. And their individualities insist that they adopt different coping strategies. Anne had heard her husband quote Yeats--"the center cannot hold"--too many times not to be concerned about the future.

What the Lindbloom clan faced locally, thought Anne, the United States was also seeing globally. While the fall of the Berlin Wall could mean the end of a Cold War, The Middle East, a region of conflict for centuries, was threatening to undo a fragile political stability put in place by European (and American) power and influence. Arab oil could not be controlled by outsiders; and the region's culture could not be made to conform to Western ideals.

She remembered a visit she, Curtis, and the Justin (less than a year old) had made to Fairfield that opened a division between siblings. They'd come down from St. Louis in a shuttle to save the parents the two-hour drive, planning on being taxied back by Carol, who was coming up from Fort Leonard Wood the next day.

Curtis was so nervous in his new role of father that he insisted on driving his father's car to the St. Louis airport at the end of their stay. Carol was to ride with them and bring the car home; so she assumed she should be behind the wheel both ways. The discussion got ugly. Why did he not trust her? Why couldn't she accept his role as responsible parent?

Anne wondered at the time what childhood event could spawned this intense rivalry--fighting over bicycles? Or tricycles? Or strollers? Men's traditional view of women clashed with women's rights; it was the privileges of marriage versus the stereotype of 'spinsterhood'; the academic world opposed a military mentality. Anne even heard her sister-in-law say with anger, "How in the world you kept your college student ass safe in Vietnam is a mystery to me."

Years later she reevaluated the fact that both brother and sister had not been back from Southeast Asia very long, one a volunteer, the other a draftee. A war that divided the nation, she concluded, had created an environment in which old family injuries could surface in unexpected places and unrecognized forms. Would the present turn out to be a similar time?

192

The family was congregating in the great room for drinks and snacks before Anne finally decided what she would offer as her FACTH story. She hoped "The Lone Wolf" wouldn't offend anyone holding strictly to an inherited core of beliefs.

Helping to organize a dessert table, she saw Louis beside the fireplace surveying the gathering with a proprietary air. After his father, she suspected, he would be the one to hold to traditional values like the idea of a pater familias. And he might resent her story.

"Louis," she said, "coming up to his side. "I'm not sure we've all said it--it's been so busy--but we're so grateful for all you and Suzanne have done to host this event. The preparations, the arrangements, everything."

"Oh, we're happy to do it. And, of course, we have the experience."

"Yes, I know. But still…do you think we'll be able to do this again next year? Not necessarily here, but at one of our homes." She saw him frown slightly.

"That's one of the things I wanted to talk about at dinner, making a plan for…um…for subsequent occasions." He scanned the room again. "We're a central location with plenty of space. And, to tell the truth, I'm not sure Mom and Dad will be able to travel too much farther in the future."

"It's hard this time of year, I know. The snow's picking up again right now, in fact. It's a white Christmas the children are enjoying but that can make seniors nervous."

As the light dimmed outside, the large patio doors became a solid grey color, not revealing what was outside or reflecting what was inside. The flat slate wall matched her mental memory of the surface of granite outcrop she'd once stared at in Virginia's Piedmont. She also recalled her unexpected encounter with a possessive male on that elemental stone.

She had colleagues who regularly offered to go with her on her field trips to survey plant species that could survive in the thin soil on top of a rock slab. But none was available that time, and she went alone. After that, she understood why she should wait for a companion.

"Outcrops are rocks that have been thrust up from below the surface of the earth," she would explain to her Lindbloom audience, some of whom, like Ethel, the marine biologist, would already know her subject. "And they're then washed by thousands of years of rain and snow. The flora that lives in such a specialized environment have often been undisturbed and unchanged for millennia. Generally, not a good place for humans like me to find food or shelter."

In the Piedmont of Georgia, North Carolina, and Virginia, southern exposure on such formations bakes the outcrop to create a kind of desert. As in the American West, cacti or cactus-like plants lie dormant for much of the year and then explode in color when rain comes. Scientists research their adaptations for many reasons.

"While I'm not eager to forecast extreme weather conditions changing the environments in which we humans thrive," Anne would admit to the family, "I do believe learning about what can survive such extremes is worthwhile. Even now these outcrops are a valuable food source for wildlife--rabbits, deer, box turtles, coyotes."

194

Like most in her generation, she'd seen the movie, *Deliverance*, a graphic depiction of crude rural men victimizing adventure-seeking city dwellers. But given that the younger cousins probably weren't ready for that kind of tale, and that the older cousins would pretend worldly indifference, the famous rape scene would not become part of her FACTH.

Still, when she talks about this particular trip to her classes, she likes to suggest unspecified dangers in the wilderness. So, there's an extended description of the hike to the site: small creeks she has to wade; forest sounds, which include no evidence of a human presence (other than her own steps, breathing, heartbeat); switchbacks and ups and downs on infrequently used trails, which can be disorienting even for experienced hikers.

In part she knows tension in any narrative creates interest--and something unexpected did occur. But she also wants to present to her students the full context of scientific research.

The film of James Dickey's novel, Anne felt, was sensational, exploiting increasingly crass public tastes. In the movie the trio of urbanites venture into deep woods that will be covered by water when a new dam is finished--it's a final look. Cut off from their familiar world of prosperity and convenience, they are confronted not just by a primitive natural environment but also by uncontrolled sexual violence. On her botanical field trip, Anne was alone with plants and miles from any humans.

"I parked at a park trailhead and was a little disturbed that there was no place to record that I would be trekking out to a site on the far perimeter of the property. But having driven several hours to get there, I was eager to finish the work; so I took off on the three-mile trail that followed a creek up into some low mountains."

The conspicuous outcrop plants in the region she was entering included such flamboyant species as the Eastern Prickly Pear Cactus and the *viguera porteri* with its orange-yellow flowers. But that day Anne wanted to inspect lichen and moss, which help break up rock to form soil in which larger species can grow. They are pioneer species, the first in the stages of succession to establish themselves in a new environment.

"When I saw him," she would say to her audience, "I froze."

She knew that, by and large, coyotes are not dangerous to humans. But some years earlier she had also read that a three-year old child was mauled in California and subsequently died. Still, an adult person, unless injured and alone, would not be vulnerable to attack.

"Of course, I assumed it was a male, though, from where I was kneeling on my hands and knees, I couldn't see."

Should she give a little shiver to underscore the general anxiety she did feel? After all, since she was here, alive and speaking, everyone had to know she had survived.

"What I saw was his open mouth--the fangs and red tongue--and what I heard was his intimidating growl."

Perhaps someone would ask, "Were you scared?" Or say, "I would have run away as fast as my two legs would carry me!" Another, "No, climb a tree. He'll go away."

Anne would admit, "I decided to freeze. I didn't want to make any sudden movements or turn my back on him. So, I became a statue. But he didn't move either. And then…"

She'd make her most dramatic pause here, not moving as if she were still in that scene.

"And then I saw the other one, to the right of the first, trotting across the outcrop."

With her students there were always a few sharp intakes of breath, slight leanings forward.

"Actually, the other could have been the male, and I might have been looking at the mother, because at the same time coyote number two came into my view, I saw two little cubs behind the first one."

"Now you're in trouble," someone might observe. "It's like a mother bear and her babies."

"I knew that some coyote pairs stay together many seasons, raising a family each year. And the male does help with raising the young. Either will do what's necessary to protect the next generation. Together they can be especially dangerous."

"Well, what did happen? How'd you get away?"

"I didn't get away: they left. The whole family trotted off the outcrop and into the woods. It was my good fortune not to be between either parent and the pups. So long as I made no threatening moves, they were not really interested in me."

"I guess that ended your solo field trips," Curtis might say. When she got back, he had made her promise, if no one else would accompany her, she would ask him.

"It did."

Unable not to be a teacher, she would conclude, "So, I offer two lessons from my FACTH: one about me; and another about social dynamics. First, I had never traveled to dangerous places, as some of you have." She looked pointedly at Carol, veteran of many overseas tours. "So I have had to accept the judgment of my children and my husband that I am sometimes Polly-Ann-ish, innocent even."

"And…"

"And in the animal kingdom, there are no universal gender roles. Sometimes males are hunters and aggressors, but other times the females. Sometimes mothers raise the young; but in other cases the fathers do the childrearing. The leader of the pack varies with species and time."

Elizabeth might be the one to ask, "Are you about to apply this principle to humans?" If she did, Anne wouldn't know if she would be angry about the idea or pleased.

"Maybe I just think we have keep all options for survival open."

Part 7: Mark

Chapter Thirty-one: Seats

Carol would be surprised but pleased when Anne acknowledged that she had been in dangerous places as much or perhaps more than others in the family. There had always been a little tension between the sisters-in-law—different philosophies, different professions, different interests—though never hostility. Still, with the prospect of taking her whole family out of the country for some years, it was reassuring to find an in-law connecting with her at this event.

Carol wouldn't hear Anne's reference to her military service, though, until later in the evening. Before then she struggled to find a theme for her own FACTH story. An hour before festivities were to start she slipped off to the cottage hoping for inspiration.

"Aren't you going the wrong way?" Mark asked her as he and the twins passed on their way back to the big house. They were muffled up against the wind.

"Be right there. Fixing my make-up."

Marian and Christie rolled their eyes. "Like she even uses make-up," they said in unison.

"Now, you know she doesn't like emotional scenes. And I think she fears we're all going to get teary-eyed during the speeches."

"We've got the score cards Sam gave out to judge you guys," said Marian. "I think that will keep things pretty sober. And neither Grandpa nor Grandma like sentimentality."

Mark agreed. "It's your Uncle Curtis I worry about. The Mid-westerner-become-Southerner can get choked up. Most of you Americans have trouble expressing your emotions."

Mark liked to tease them that he remained Mexican at heart and that he'd had to restrain his Latin warmth in this family—handshakes rather than hugs, pecks on the cheek not kisses, avoidance of terms of affection. Everybody wanted to keep some distance.

"Well, Daddy," cautioned Christie, "be sure you're under control then. We'll signal you if we suspect you're about to go touchy-feely on us."

He laughed, but he worried that discord, not sentiment, might emerge this evening. He'd overhead Curtis asking about seating for the dinner and Suzanne reporting what Louis had decided. Curtis would be at the smaller table and his older brother opposite their father at the two ends of the main table. She insisted that there was no "kid's table." But Mark watched his brother-in-law scowl at this explanation.

Of course, this was Louis' house, the restored and refurbished Overton mansion. And someone should emcee the evening's events. But Mark noted Curtis' displeasure and later mentioned it to Carol. She shrugged, saying simply "Men."

He had heard her talk bitterly about the Paris Peace Accords of twenty years ago and wondered if she was repressing parallels. Representatives of the parties in the Vietnam War—all men—debated the shape of and seating at the proposed negotiation table. Thousands more Americans would die, and many more Vietnamese, as the political posturing went on in one of the great capitals of the West.

At the time, working fields in the San Joaquin valley and trying to get a college degree one course at a time,

Mark (originally "Marcos") had not been concerned with that faraway conflict. He'd spent his early childhood with parents, cousins, and grandparents in a two-room adobe house on a dairy farm and believed that people had to learn to accommodate each other if they meant to survive as a community. He often used the example of the honeybee ready to die to protect the hive to make this point.

His family in Chihuahua kept bees that fertilized desert cactus; those plants in turn provided food for dairy cows on land that was close to barren. In years when water was especially sparse, the beekeepers would burn spines off the cactus in a process called "chamuscando" so that cattle could eat the pads for food and water. A fragile chain of dependency connected the bees to the cactus to the cows to the people. Anything that upset any element of this interdependency could mean the collapse of the whole.

Over the years some bee colonies simply disappeared, whether killed by virus, poor nutrition, stress, or environmental damage through such things as pesticide use, no one knew. But without resources other than their own labor, farmers and beekeepers sometimes had to leave the land they loved and look for new opportunities elsewhere. That's how Marcos came to America and became Mark, though there were still times he returned mentally to his childhood self.

In the great room, Mark was quickly confronted by his daughters. "They've got us organized by families, but the girls want to sit with each other."

"Is that so you can whisper and pass notes about the old folks?" he teased.

Marian huffed. "Well, in anticipation of the FACTH competition, we need to share our opinions about

202

everyone. While you're not going to shush us, Mom might. And the boys—they're already rebelling. You need to talk to Uncle Louis. Or to Grandma."

"Maybe you're old enough to take some of these things on for yourselves. Get with your cousin Sam. He's a pretty forceful arguer and a bit of a diplomat. He might even be able to do something without getting everybody upset."

He saw Carol coming toward them and raised his eyebrows, an understood distress sign. Miriam and Marian saw it, too, and slipped off with a conspiratorial look.

Mark quickly explained the table placement issues. As he expected, Carol was not interested in confronting her brothers unnecessarily, having done that enough when they were children. And she had her own worry.

"Our nephew, Ben, surprised me just a minute ago by asking what it had been like to introduce a…a 'person from another culture,' I believe is the way he put it—into this family."

"Ah. So Elizabeth is from another culture?"

"I hadn't thought so, but you know how we have so many hyphenated Americans these days, as well as individuals identified by religious denominations or generational categories. Maybe she's 'military American,' daughter of an Army general."

"Or 'upper crust' American or 'East Coast' American. I can see that it might be hard to adjust to the Lindbloom professional Midwestern class. What did you tell him?"

"I actually felt that Ben never thought about the fact that you're Mexican, or Mexican-American, until recently. I mean, I'm sure Louis told him a long time ago, but, meeting you, there's little except your appearance—and that's not a dead giveaway—that says 'Hispanic.'"

"Perhaps. And now as he watches his wife's somewhat standoffish behavior here, her obvious allegiance to her own family, he's wondering if he can keep his close relationship to his parents and siblings the way you have."

Carol shrugged. "My family had more problems with me than with you! But, by the way, that's another of the advantages of being in the military—you're organized, at least on the surface, by rank and specialty, not by race or culture. And when you go overseas, you rely on any kind of hyphenated American."

Sam, rattling a spoon against a glass, interrupted all conversation in a loud voice, "We have a problem."

His father said, "Problem? Nothing we can't sort out over dinner, I'm sure."

The other cousins had materialized around Sam, apparently their spokesman.

"It's not serious, but we feel..." he waved at his smiling cousins, "we feel we need to make a few adjustments before we all take our seats for the big event. You see, Mother—whom I love dearly—overlooked one factor that will make dining more comfortable this evening."

Suzanne looked puzzled, but apparently used to her son's flair for the dramatic, not hurt. Louis, however, frowned.

"You see, there are seven left-handers in this assembly. Being one myself, I know it can be awkward if we're a bit crowded and sitting next to a right-hander."

204

"Nothing wrong with being right-handed, of course," Justin added. "The fair Abigail, for instance," winking at his girlfriend, "is…um, 'that way.'" Snickers from the older cousins.

"So," continued Sam, "we've shifted the two tables slightly, maybe 15 degrees, and made a few simple adjustments to the seating chart. In fact, you'll see that Grandma has already rearranged the place cards, so that left-handers will not be bumping elbows with right-handers."

Since no one was able to raise an objection (though Louis continued to frown), they all left their hors d'ouerves plates and drink classes and went into the dining room. Mark noted how neatly the cousins ended up close enough to talk to each other. And if it were possible, the space seemed more open. Later Mark would recall this scene as the lull before the storm.

Chapter Thirty-two: Thanks

The joyous invasion of the dining room by Dorothy, escape artist schnauzer, was the first—but not the last—of the evening's disturbances. Zipping around the table and human legs, she dodged efforts to catch her and made an heroic leap at the steaming roast beef platter on the sideboard. Louis' anger was barely contained. "Ben! Sam! Get that dog out of here."

His older son responded with some resentment, "She was locked in the utility room."

Dorothy careened off the sideboard and slid across the polished wood floor. But, back on her feet, she was circling for another attempt when Justin's Abigail scooped her up. Dorothy happily licked her face. Abigail kept control of her and carried her back to the utility room.

"Good job, Abby," said Justin, following her. Over his shoulder he muttered, "Maybe now *some* people in this family will be a little nicer to my girlfriend." Mark was not the only one to raise an eyebrow, though the cousins generally looked down at their plates.

When they returned and everyone had settled back down, Louis rose to say grace: "Bless us, Oh Lord, and these thy gifts, which we are about to receive, from thy bounty, through Christ, Our Lord." All responded, "Amen."

As everyone unfolded their napkins and started to chat, Carol rose. "If it's okay, I'd like to offer a second prayer, one appropriate to Christmas. It was given by Astronaut Frank Borman on the 1968 Apollo 8 space mission and seems relevant to the time we live in, to the new year with its challenges."

Mark noted, again, that Louis frowned.

"Let us pray. 'Give us, O God, the vision which can see your love in the world in spite of human failure. Give us the faith to trust your goodness in spite of our ignorance and weakness. Give us the knowledge that we may continue to pray with understanding hearts. And show us what each one of us can do to set forward the coming of the day of universal peace."

There was quiet for a few seconds. Then Sam said, "Well, Aunt Carol, you've sure sobered us up. But, if it's okay, we'll go ahead and enjoy this feast."

She smiled and raised her glass to him.

Mark knew what had inspired his wife: she had been hearing from her connections in military intelligence about the likelihood America would soon be at war again. He also knew most of the rest of this group would see the Iraq-Kuwait situation as unconnected to themselves and their futures. That was the other side of the world.

Mark sat across from the girl cousins, Ethel and Mary Ann, and next to Sam. His two girls were on the other side of Sam, so Mark could see how members of the younger generation were able to communicate with each other over, around, and behind their parents.

Ethel caught his eye, smiled, and said, "Mi universidad es muy interesante." Sliding her bread plate to one side so she could put her glass on her left, she added. "Ahora estoy estudiando Español. En Florida hay muchas personas latinoamericanos." *My university is very interesting. I'm studying Spanish. In Florida there are many Latin American people.*

"Muy bien," Mark said. "Estoy aprendiendo alemán porque mi negocio tiene clientes en Europa. Sprechen sie Deutsch?" *Very good. I'm learning German because my business has many customers en Europe. Do you speak German?*

"Lo siento. Un peu de français." *No, sorry. A little French.*

"Your aunt learned French in the Army for her tours in Southeast Asia."

Ethel leaned closer to confess that maybe they should speak English now so as not to appear to be outsiders. Then, seeing the servings being passed, she said "I guess they have a veggie option for the twins."

"There's a meatless lasagna, which I'm having. My daughters have changed my diet!"

Conversation was suspended as plates were passed and two kinds of rolls, cranberries, butter, and other condiments traveled the different tables. Right-handers and left-handers shifted a few dishes around, but soon all were enjoying the meal without elbowing each other.

A few minutes later, Ethel looked at her plate and back at the sideboard. "When I see what's happening in agriculture—concentrated beef and chicken production—I'm inclined to follow my cousins' meatless way, too. Those giant chicken houses, thousands of square feet, and the birds so thick in there they cover the floor, beak to tail."

"Actually, not beak to tail, as they're 'de-beaked' early," corrected Mark. "The 'farmers'--if I can use the term loosely--slice off the chicks' beaks when they're young so they won't peck each other to death."

She grimaced. "We have to sacrifice some animals in the laboratory in the interest of science; so I'm not drawing absolute lines. But cooped up like that, I can see why the chickens go crazy—stir crazy, I guess."

208

"My family used to raise them when we first came to America. Chickens know each other, communicating with chirps and crowing, and they form a hierarchy in small groups. I used to like watching them dust bathing all together. It's recreation for them."

Images of those years came to his mind, some pleasant but others less so. The chickens were prone to disease; there were predators who seemed always able to get under or over fences; prices to buy would go up, to sell down. It had been a hard life in the crowded immigrant neighborhood. He attributed his parents' early deaths to the physical strains of labor and less than healthful environmental conditions.

Ethel said. "Some call those production sheds 'Broiler-chicken factories.'"

"It is sad. The birds can't do what their ancestors have always done: roam, scratch in the dirt, socialize. They end up fighting in tight quarters, even with no beaks."

"There's a lot of new literature about all this, not just about how it's cruel to animals, but it also causes environmental damage."

"'Fowling your own nest,' to recall the literal meaning of that phrase."

She grinned and waved off the basket of rolls coming around the table a second time. "I need to be careful about crowding my stomach; the food's all so good. And rumor has it that we have every kind of dessert known to humankind."

"You're a slim young woman and being active will keep you that way." He paused to take a sip of wine. "Another bad feature of the food industry is penning up livestock. Your dad told me about passing one of those beef cattle 'feedlots' in Kansas last year, when he was visiting some of Grandpa's childhood homes."

"Oh, yes. Father said they could smell it long before they saw the packed…lot—you couldn't call it a pasture. The cattle were eating specialized food and pooping at the same time, standing in their own feces."

At the other table Louis tapped a spoon on his wine glass and rose. "As you all continue to enjoy God's bounty, let me say how pleased Suzanne and I are that the entire family has been able to be together for the first time in…well, in quite some time."

Mark saw some eyes widen at the prospect of an extended speech before the official giving of toasts scheduled with dessert.

"What the future holds for the Lindblooms—and," Louis smiled at his daughter-in-law, "those who will be Lindblooms—we cannot say for sure. But I want to assure you all that the Overton Estate will remain a gathering point for many years. I feel it's my role to encourage these reunions."

Mark thought he was about to announce himself "the first-born son," heir apparent to a throne, and worried that Curtis might question this vision.

Instead, Grandpa interrupted to say, "Now, Fairfield is still a fine place to visit. It's where you three grew up," he waved to his children. "You still have friends there. And that reminds me how pleasant it was to travel back to my boyhood home last summer." Again Mark saw eyes widen.

Mid tapped him on the arm. "We all give our stories once we have dessert. You need to save your tale of the high climbing Oswald for just a bit longer."

"Oh," Oscar said, seeming deflated. "I was going to mention a different...um, person. Babs McCauley," he added with sudden energy. "*She* was a daring girl!"

Suzanne rose and asked everyone to please take their plates to the kitchen and return with desserts and more drinks. "Then," she smiled at Grandpa," it will be time for the toasts."

Mark knew Carol's mother hid her feelings well; but he had seen her exchange a look of concern with Suzanne. Just as the wind was howling outside the mansion, so it appeared spirits were unsettled inside it.

Chapter Thirty-three: Bombshells

The last to come back from the kitchen was Curtis who, standing behind his chair with a piece of pecan pie on a plate in one hand, a coffee cup in the other, nodded toward his father and told the group, "I'd like to agree with Grandpa. We should keep all options for future gatherings open."

Mark saw Louis frown yet again.

Smiling, Curtis explained, "I even wonder if we might think about a 'destination vacation' together. You know, we would choose a site we'd all like to visit—New Orleans, Quebec, maybe even the Bahamas. It would take a lot of planning, but…it would be exciting."

"I've liked being in a whole new place," offered Ethel. "Florida has so much to see, like the Keys, the Everglades, the Gulf Coast."

Elizabeth asserted, "All of you could learn a lot in Boston, where our nation was founded. And Nantucket is a wonderful vacation spot."

Mark leaned back and watched the discussion spread, as person after person insisted they had "always wanted to see X" or wondered, "what would it be like to go to Y?" It wasn't clear how many were seriously interested in the idea of meeting each other in one of those places so much as the thought gave them an opportunity to talk about travel adventure.

As the general discussion broke up into smaller groups, each talking about past trips and dream journeys, the tension subsided. Louis' implied assertion that everyone should think of his home as the family's central location was not directly challenged, but it had certainly not been endorsed.

Mark would have liked to propose they all meet in Mexico, perhaps Guadalajara, closest big city to where he'd grown up and rich in culture. But even if some were interested in going south of the border, it would probably be to a beach resort like Cancun or Acapulco.

He looked at Carol, who sat across from Curtis at the "not grown-ups" table. She was quiet, which was not unusual; and he guessed she was trying to mentally go over her FACTH story. But he also knew she'd taken so many overseas trips she was probably not excited about travel to what the others would think of as an exotic location.

Mark also knew she planned to announce in just a few minutes that her branch of the family would be spending at least the next two years in Europe. Cellular telephone service was advancing into new, expanding markets; and Mark felt he had personally to broker cooperative relationships with foreign companies.

In recent years, he'd traveled a fair amount back to Mexico and around different places in both Central and South America, assessing the future for his business. Expansion there, he felt, would lag behind what was happening in Asia and Europe; but the speed of innovation in the communication industry was often greater than predicted by investors. The software designers and computer builders belonged to a new generation that thought big and moved fast.

He'd also gone to Spain when Carol was stationed in Germany and again more recently. They'd billed that later trip as a vacation and taken the girls, but Mark was also exploring his family's history. He was surprised at discoveries he made in a remote village in the Basque region.

Mark's grandmother had talked about her grandfather, with whom the family had lost touch in the middle of the nineteenth-century. The sketchy details handed down to later generations contained an anecdote about this Spanish immigrant's remarkable ability to move bee colonies.

According to the legend, Enrique would slowly approach a bee colony. With no protective clothing, singing a Spanish lullaby, he would slip a woven basket under the hive, lift it, and carry it to a new home as far as several miles away. He never received a sting. It was believed that in his lifetime he spread bees throughout a valley over one hundred miles long.

He was also said he spread his own seed throughout the villages along the river. A handsome man with an exotic, foreign air, he was enamored by so many maidens and some wives that families in many places claimed kinship with the man who could charm bees.

Most of the stories about Enrique asserted that he was from a tiny village, Villanueva de Puerta, in the north of Spain. On a whim, Mark toured the area asking about the González family.

Of course, he heard many accounts of famous ancestors, some of whom had left to start over in distant lands. In one instance a village ancient claimed that she had heard about a man who could mesmerize bees and women.

"He was a handsome one like you," the senior claimed. "He was also a traveling musician who played the guitar and sang lullabies at the windows of young girls. They would lose all power of resistance and invite him into their beds."

214

"Ah, Abuela," Mark laughed. "Are you telling me the truth?"

She flashed a toothy grin as if she had been one of Enrique's lovers herself. "Si, señor. I always tell the truth…unless a falsehood will do better."

Mark couldn't tell whether the man she remembered might be remotely related to him, or if he was more a fiction than a memory. But he was amused to find himself treated as if he were himself a long lost son of the region.

Families insisted he eat with them, introduced him (in fact, a very attractive man) to their daughters, invited him to stay with them for as long as he wished. While his Spanish differed from theirs—and was, in fact, sometimes rusty without use—he felt he had been embraced by the community.

As the Lindbloom family debated the clan's future, Mark took an optimistic view that what they shared was as strong as the sense of kinship linking him to the people of Villanueva de Puerta.

Still, he recognized that any plan for another Lindbloom reunion was complicated enough with everyone in one country. His being overseas with Carol and the twins would multiply the variables. And who was to say more family members wouldn't be abroad in another year's time? Just as important, would they find that their different interests and paths toward fulfillment were pulling them apart more than kinship drew them together?

Then Grandpa put the discussion in a more somber mode. "Actually," he said with an odd look on his face, "Fairfield may not be so good a place for a reunion as I indicated earlier. I'm…um…contemplating some changes."

"Changes?" Curtis asked.

"Yes, yes, changes. Mid and I…well, we have not been doing so well lately…and, to tell the truth, I'm thinking . . .well, I'm the one not doing so well…with memory . . ."

Mid interrupted. "Oscar, we agreed that we wouldn't talk about that right now. It spoils the holiday."

Carol said sharply, "We should hear a little of this right now."

Mid sighed. "He's having some tests, that's all. As we age, we all have problems with short-term memory. I'm taking the tests, too. It's nothing to worry about."

"Yes, yes," muttered Oscar, examining his plate as if it held some sort of clue. "And the falling…well, I guess I have to admit that I've lost half a step. But I am," he brightened, "I am approaching eighty years of age, you know."

"Oh, we both are, Oscar. But we're doing just fine."

Their children and their spouses knew that Grandma was some years older than Oscar. While she was spry for her age, she could not handle all the household chores without some help. And because of cataracts, she liked for him to do the driving, especially at night.

What Louis said next, closed off conversation abruptly. "I've made some inquiries at several good facilities in the St. Louis area. I'll make sure you are well taken care of."

Chapter Thirty-four: Hexagons

As they got ready for bed, Mark said to Carol, "I have a feeling Louis and Curtis have not exactly kept you in the loop about your parents' health."

"Affirmative, but no surprise. They've always thought Dad is immune to aging."

She was doing her usual toe-touches. They would be followed by sit-ups and push-ups—her nightly routine.

Mark hung his shirt on the back of a chair. "I didn't like the look on your mother's face. She usually hides her emotions, but Oscar's announcement caught her by surprise."

He'd also surveyed other faces at both tables. The older grandchildren looked concerned, the younger ones puzzled. Sam was struck.

Dropping to do her twenty, Carol said, "I couldn't get Suzanne alone, but tomorrow we'll have a talk. She is alert to such things and more forthcoming."

He stretched out on the bed. "You know, if you think you're going have to be in Fairfield to take care of things, we can work something out."

Rolling onto her back and hooking her toes under the bedrail, she moved on to sit-ups. When she had first retired, Mark thought she took her workout routines too seriously. Each week, more time was added to each session, new muscles were worked.

She said, "We have reservations to fly back we should keep. Let's not leap to conclusions. Curtis and Louis aren't completely incompetent."

Mark knew by her tone, however, that she was uneasy. He would have to watch out that her anxiety didn't get channeled into other avenues, like increasing the girls' swimming training. She'd gotten control of her own exercise regimen only when she was comfortable about work and family.

As they'd considered living overseas in the last few months, he saw signs in her workout: slight increases in time and speed meant that she was processing issues. He concluded that a desire to be more in contact with the rest of her family was one of the causes of her extended exercises.

Carol's early tours abroad had been exciting and fulfilling. But as she approached the twenty-year mark in her career, she began to complain about feeling cut off from her parents, siblings, nieces, and nephews.

He remembered his parents as he was finishing high school in California; they longed to be in touch with relatives back in Chihuahua. But money was tight and they couldn't afford to travel often. Then his mother's sudden illness and his father's rapid decline afterwards prevented the reconnections both had wanted.

He was grateful for his own success in their adopted country, which had given him the means to travel. He'd taken his younger sisters, born in this country, to Mexico several times and reacquainted himself with relatives he knew mostly by name from his parents' tales. Each year, his own business made communication with them easier.

Still, he'd spent most of his life in the United States and was grateful for the opportunities it had given him. His real family was here.

"Remember the first time you brought me home with you?" he asked Carol as she climbed into bed.

218

"Of course."

"Everyone kind of looked at me out of the corners of their eyes, trying to figure me out without being too conspicuous about it."

"I hadn't said much about you. Just that we'd met at the gym and that you were in the telephone business."

"Your dad started this academic conversation about radio waves and electronic impulses, how they're similar but different. His speech and my speech were like that, each moving through its own medium with different pulses and pauses and not connecting at many points."

She laughed. "Was that when he started quizzing you about your family? He'd had little idea of California or the West beyond what he'd read in John Steinbeck and Zane Grey."

"And I gave an evasive account of them as 'farmers.' I didn't say 'farm workers' or 'itinerate agricultural laborers.' He launched into tales of prairie wheat and hot, dry wind blowing dust across Kansas towns in the Depression."

"Humph. The more you two talked, the more both of you diverged from each other and from the truth."

"Eventually, though, he came to see me as an engineer, a self-made man. And that's what he is too, having had few advantages except his natural wit to bring him up from the previous generation of carpenters and builders."

Mark admired his father-in-law, though he felt that recently Oscar airbrushed complications from his pictures of the world. Mark believed in a strict connection between the abstract and the concrete, the world of ideas and the physical universe. From their first meeting, he had admired Carol's ability to integrate programming skills with direct experience. To guide a missile from launch to landing by code—and then predict the effects on a distant target—you must have a solid grasp of reality.

He'd seen Carol's skill in connecting theory to practice last summer when she responded to her daughters' request for science fair topics.

"Well, you know water expands when it freezes, right?" she asked. They were having a Saturday morning lunch out after a swim meet.

They nodded, but he suspected they were going to learn why as well as how.

"Water's molecular structure is such that it forms hexagons when it drops below 4° Celsius." She drew the shape on a paper napkin. Mark worried she was going to write equations for the process. "And this shape contains more space than H_2O in its liquid state."

"Let's check this out with milkshakes," offered Christie.

"It's not part of your training diet, but maybe your dad will eat one, and we'll watch to see if it gets smaller in his mouth."

"Ewww," said Marian

"Of course," Carol went on, "you'd have experienced this if you'd grown up in Grandma's house, as I did. We didn't have an icemaker. Can you believe that?"

"You had to drink Coke warm?"

"Oh, we had ice. It's just that we had to make our own by pouring water into a tray divided into little sections, one for each ice cube-to-be. We put the tray into the freezer section of our refrigerator and waited for it to freeze."

"Lucky you," exclaimed Mark. "You *had* a refrigerator!"

Both girls wagged a finger at him. They were used to his exaggerating the hardships of his childhood. "We know, we know. All you had was a picture of the North Pole cut from a magazine you swiped from a rich man's garbage can."

"Yes, until I left it out in the sun one day, and it burst into flames."

"Back to the lesson at hand," insisted Carol. "So, if you want ice on a warm afternoon, what should you do in the morning?"

"Fill the ice tray thingie and put it in the freezer?"

"Right. Fill them just a little bit, or all the way to the top? You want lots, as it's going to be as hot as the desert in Chihuahua."

The girls didn't fall for the trap. "Halfway," said Marian. "So it won't expand and slop over the edges."

Christie squinted at her mother as if she had now become the teacher. "You see, with its hexagonal shape, water grows as it freezes."

"Very good. Now, here's one more tidbit about that iceberg your father supposedly had a picture of way back in his childhood. Because the ice, with more empty space, is lighter than water, it floats on top of any ocean, river, lake. And because what freezes rises to the top, making a cap, the rest of the iceberg forms beneath it. Usually what you see floating in the ocean is a giant ice mass with nine-tenths of it hidden. What we see of an iceberg, then, is only a small portion of the whole thing."

As Mark remembered that science lesson, he realized that, at this holiday gathering, they might be seeing only the tip of the family's problems.

Chapter Thirty-five: Bees

"I need you to tell Dad about the pipe shop you visited in Malmo," Carol said to Mark, referring to an event on a business trip to Scandinavia.

He was almost asleep, but rose up to say, "He knows more about pipes than anybody. What am I going to say, that they had meerschaum and briar pipes, big bowls, little bowls, long stems, short stems?"

"Whatever. You just get him started, and he'll probably take it from there. The idea is to keep him occupied for a couple of hours tomorrow afternoon. I'm going to organize a summit, the next generation. We need to confront Mom and find out exactly what's going on with Dad…well, with the two of them."

"Ah, I'm the diversion, then, not a team member."

"I'll tell you everything that's said. You'll have some distance, hearing it at one remove as well as being one of the outlaws. I'd have you there, but you're the only one I can count on to do the job of occupying Dad. After all, mister telephone maker, you're an expert on expanding conversation across time and space."

"Humph. That's true, though a lot of the time I fear I'm not adding anything significant to the world's talk."

"Ask him about famous pipe smokers. You'll hear about Einstein, McCarther, Mark Twain. He claims Sherlock Holmes isn't the only one who sits in an easy chair and fills the room with a cloud of inspiration."

The picture made Mark recall the (literally) smoky back room of that little shop in Sweden he'd ducked into out of curiosity. He learned there, among other things, that a number of famous women, like George Sand and Virginia Woolf, had been pipe smokers. He'd never thought about it before, but tobacconists probably saw the advantage of including them in their clientele—more customers.

The shop owner, not a characteristically taciturn Swede, seemed to take it as a special mission to convince Mark that pipe smoking was a fine (and healthy) tradition. He did so in the Queen's English, proud of his skill (probably unaware than Mark was bilingual as well).

Acknowledging the 1970s campaign to curb cigarette smoking, Lars explained that the tobacco industry believed the pipe was a healthy alternative (which, Mark realized, meant the business saw potential for an expanded market). You don't inhale, was the idea; but Mark suspected more restrictions were in the air (he grinned at the double meaning, which might have escaped the Swede).

In the long run, he believed, education would do more than legal action to change people's habits. If they understood the consequences of their actions, many would become their own police. He believed this because school had been his way up and out of limited circumstances, and not just in California. He'd learned from stories told by parents and grandparents in his native Mexico.

When he had his talk—more of a listen—with Oscar, he realized he had an educational Far Away Close to Home story already in his possession.

When Marcos was a child, four or five years old, he decided that there were too may bees in one of the hives his father tended. Having seen them swarm and leave a hive before with no apparent harm, he pushed one box over and said half would need to leave. Of course, he was stung and ran screaming to his father.

Miguel, who had been bitten so many times he no longer noticed, sat down with his son and told him a story about bees. Marcos/Mark, in turn, later told his daughters. Now he would tell the larger family.

"Many, many years ago, before you were born, before any of us where born, in a beautiful forest up in the mountains a very old man lived with his very old wife. They could talk to the animals who shared the woods with them—the rabbits, the deer, the bears."

Marcos, the child, had wondered, "The bears!"

"Yes, the birds and the mice and even the bears. There was enough for all in this land, so no one wanted what others had. They enjoyed the berries growing on bushes, the nuts that fell from trees, plants that had soft stems and tasty leaves."

"No one had to work?" Like his cousins, Marcos had been given chores as soon as he had the ability to perform them. He fed chickens, sorted limberbush for making baskets, stirred the water in the pot in which clothes were washed.

"They did have to work, but this was back when the world was young, and the earth, our mother, gave people much that they needed. Now, this old couple had a small boy—a boy about as old as you are. They said his coming to them in their later years was a miracle. But because his parents were so old, and they lived by themselves in the forest, the boy didn't have any brothers or sisters to play with, and he was sad."

"Oh-uh!" Marcos had heard enough stories to suspect the boy would do something and get in trouble for it.

His father went on. "The boy was watching bees fly down into the garden, drink the nectar from the flowers, then fly away. And he could hear them talking, telling each other where the best plants were and which flowers were now empty. They seemed so happy together."

"Did they see the boy and sting him?"

"They saw him, but they were a kind of bee that didn't sting. They found their homes in fallen logs of dense forests. So they didn't have to build their own."

Carlos' family had been beekeepers for generations and could trace many of their practices back to the Mayans, for whom stingless species were part of their religious culture.

He went on. "They let all the creatures of the forest share their honey. Watching them fly away, the boy envied the beautiful, happy, honey-making bees who had so many friends."

"I bet he wished he could go with them."

"You're right. And, since the bees could talk and understand humans, one of them asked the boy, 'Do you want to learn to fly and come away with us?'"

"'Oh yes,' said the boy, 'please let me go with you and have many friends.'"

It was believed that bees were messengers between the living world and the spirit world. In tropical southern Mexico, the people harvested honey from large-bodied bees, believing honey to be a gift of the spirit.

The father told Marcos, "The bee then said to the boy, 'if you come with us, you will be able to fly. But you will not be able to come back and live with your people because you will become a bee like us.'"

The Europeans introduced Africanized honeybees to the New World. They sting but produce much more honey than native species. Beekeepers saw the advantages of raising them in hives they could build and maintain; and the native bees then had to compete with the more aggressive introduced species. Over time, the stingless bees died out. Rituals and legends associated with Mayan customs lingered in many families, but the ancient bee-keeping practices themselves faded.

"What did the boy do?" asked Marcos, rubbing several of the sore places on his arm and looking out across the field to be sure no bees were close.

"He flew away with the bees. Although it was crowded in their log nest, they found room for him. And he had many friends."

"But he never saw his parents again?"

"Well, it turned out that, on two days each year, he could fly back and talk to them. Because they could never tell which was their son until he spoke, they protected every bee. And they lived the rest of their lives in great happiness."

"So, maybe one of the bees who chased after me was the boy who could fly."

"It's possible. Did you try to talk to him?"

Marcos laughed. "I was too busy running!"

"Do see why what you did was wrong?"

Marcos frowned. "If I'm supposed to protect the bees, I guess I'll have to let them all stay. But I wish they would teach me to fly, too."

Now president of his own company and able to travel around the world, he realized the bees that were part of his family's livelihood in Mexico had taught him to fly. But he knew he would always return to his family. And he felt that those he loved were talking to him wherever he traveled.

Part 8: Carol

Before the grand consortium of Oscar and Mid's children and their spouses was convened, a smaller group came together. Benjamin had told his mother he was worried about Elizabeth and the pregnancy. Suzanne told Carol who decided to get all the women together to discuss the situation.

"Don't you just mean you, me, Anne, and Mother—the mothers?" asked Suzanne. They were in the pantry checking supplies. Some of the family were leaving later that afternoon and the others soon thereafter.

"Oh, these issues shouldn't be kept secret, 'old wives' tales.' I suspect there's nothing to worry about, and it might be educational for the daughters."

She knew Suzanne was more old-school, cautious in talking about what used to be called "women's problems." But Carol, as usual, had an agenda—and this was only a part of it.

In the kitchen, she found Marian scrounging in the refrigerator for an energy drink and said, "Get your sister, Ethel, Lucy, Mary Anne, and Abigail together in…um…the library. I'll round up Aunt Anne and Grandma."

"What? Now? We're in the final stages of Clue." The cousins loved the board game, though locating the pieces in the rec room closet had been an unusual challenge. A Sunday school class Suzanne taught had been the last to use it; and in putting things away they'd scrambled the pieces of several games in different boxes and drawers.

"Can you wind it up in thirty minutes, Miss Scarlett-in-the-Kitchen-with-a-Poker?"

Her daughter huffed. "You know there's no poker—revolver, knife, iron pipe, candlestick, wrench, and rope are the murder weapons. But, yes, *some*one you know and love. . . " she winked, "is about to identify the killer, the location of the attack, and the weapon used." She skipped out with the drink in one hand, the other showing a thumbs up.

The reference to the popular board game reminded Suzanne that Curtis had once again hidden clues to the Two-son Riddle around the house.

When the the family gathered—in the past, that had generally been at Grandpa and Grandma's in Fairfield—Curtis identified a theme to their many conversations and hid clues to a related memorable phrase around the house.

On one occasion his nephew Sam had amused all the adults by insisting that "when I grew up, you'll grow down." It led to discussions about the challenges of being young and small, but also of being old and big. So, Curtis announced his riddle: "How did we witness Newton's third law of motion—for every action there is an equal and opposite reaction?"

He placed hints to the solution on numbered slips of paper strategically placed around the house—under the sugar bowl, on top of the television, in Grandma's sewing basket. Each piece of paper contained a key to the riddle, usually made up of pictures: 1) a clock (for "when"), 2) an eye (for "I"), 3) a beanstalk (for "grow up"), etc.

Of course, Curtis' selection of the central topic was declared arbitrary, and some others complained his solution too academic. But the family (except for Oscar) loved games, and Two-son Riddle provided a way to think through and remember what their time together meant. Curtis' riddle this time was "Who wins the battle of the sexes?"

The discussion of Elizabeth's condition was, unfortunately less jovial. With the ten women settled in the library, Carol explained that Elizabeth had had some spotting.

"It's not that unusual at this stage of a pregnancy," admitted Suzanne. "But naturally she's concerned. That's why she's in her room again right now."

Abigail was clearly uncomfortable. "I think…um…that this is a private, family matter," and started to get up.

Carol held up a hand. "These things used to be hush-hush, but women's health isn't something to be embarrassed about. Please stay."

"But you're not going to invite the men to this discussion," asserted Lucy.

Ethel insisted that "there would be nothing wrong with that. But my sense is that Aunt Carol wants the women to share first."

Carol smiled at her niece and nodded. "I know the older males wouldn't want to be here. And we don't need to make more of this than it is. Plus, because Elizabeth doesn't seem to like everyone talking about her, we'll keep the talk somewhat limited."

Suzanne concurred. "This kind of attention makes her nervous, and she doesn't want to disturb our last day together."

"She and Ben are excited, I know," said Mid, "and this is also a bit scary. So the first question is, do they want to see a doctor?"

Suzanne said, "It's not that much. And we all know it isn't unusual."

232

"Any pain, discomfort?" asked Anne.

"No. Just a little of what I see as morning sickness."

Mid: "So, wait and see?"

"Nature does have her way," observed Anne. She taught human physiology in her general biology course, giving the next generation a lot more information than she and her siblings had received in their youth about the reproductive process.

Seeing general agreement in the faces around her, Carol asked Suzanne, "Has she called *her* mother?"

"She's reluctant to do that. I'm not exactly sure why…"

"Hmm. I don't want us to be taking the place of her family."

They saw her point. Connecting two sets of parents who would share grandchildren was a complicated process. They had to be sure they weren't asserting too large a role as Liz's in-laws. Mid agreed to be mediator, contacting the Staffords herself if it proved necessary. But for now it was watch and wait. Suzanne would go up to reassure Elizabeth in just a few moments.

Then Carol said, "The *other* thing I wanted to talk about…" The pause was rhetorical. "Mark and I are moving overseas. And, if Dad is beginning to have serious health issues, I don't want the women of the family necessarily to be the only ones responsible for taking care of him. Well," she nodded at Mid, "and of Mom."

Suzanne said, "But our husbands work, and we will have the time."

Anne pointed out, "I have a full-time job, Carol probably has two. Ethel's preparing for a career; things are different than when we were young."

Mary Anne agreed. "All my classmates plan on college and a professional life. The boys understand that.

"But they won't shoulder the tasks women have traditionally taken on," insisted Carol. "The housekeeping, cooking, supervising children."

Suzanne sighed. "Now that you say it, I've done those things since I was a teenager, the oldest of six. Then I married Louis—not that I regret it!—and Benjamin came along quickly, and then the others. I have a lifetime of nursing patients through childhood illnesses."

Mid pointed out. "But to be honest, you'd be the one everyone expects to drive down to Fairfield. Not," she raised a finger, "that there's necessarily going to be a…an immediate need." Her voice trailed off, and she had a wistful look on her face.

"If you need us, though," insisted Lucy, "we'll all pitch in."

Mid's look softened, but she added. "Of course, you all know I'm somewhat older than Grandpa."

"Well," concluded Carol, rising. "The men in our family are perfectly capable. They just need…they need a bit of education on certain topics. Which will be a job for all of us." There were smiles all around, and the twins giggled.

At that moment Sam burst into the room. "First Two-Son Riddle clue!" he announced, waving a piece of paper. "Just found it held down by the television remote."

The younger girls gathered around him. "It's a picture of Albert Einstein," said Mary Anne. "What does that mean?"

"Is there more?" asked Christie. Sam turned the sheet over to reveal the picture of a nose.

"Einstein's nose?" wondered Marian. "Does he sniff out nature's secrets?"

Carol frowned. "You can do better than that. What was Einstein?"

"A genius," said several.

And then Anne laughed. Tapping her finger several times on her nose, she announced, "A wise man knows…something."

Chapter Thirty-seven: Snapshots

When Sam found his grandfather lying on the bedroom floor, it was too much like an eerie manifestation of the solution to the latest game of Clue: "with a candlestick in the study." The little table by his easy chair knocked over, the lampshade rolled away, and the gold stem angled off to one side. Sam screamed at the red stain by Oscar's head.

Half a dozen family members were there in a seconds. Carol waved everyone back except Mid.

Oscar was conscious but confused. It appeared that he had gotten up too quickly, become dizzy and fell, knocking over the table. The red stain came from a glass of cranberry juice he'd been drinking.

"What…why are you all in here?" Oscar asked with a puzzled look.

Carol responded, "The question is what are you doing lying on the floor, Dad?"

He raised his head. "On the floor? I thought I was in bed." He looked at Mid and then scanned the room. "Ah, I suspect what happened is that I got up out of the chair too fast. Must have lost my balance. It…it can happen."

Carol looked at her mother, whose face suggested that this wasn't the first time he'd fallen. "Lie back, Dad. Let me see if you're bleeding anywhere. Do you think you broke anything?"

"No, no. Look." He waved both arms, lifted his legs from the rug; but his face was pale.

"He goes down the right way," Mid explained. "Sort of sinks rather than toppling backwards or onto his face."

236

Curtis said, "Still, he should be more careful." He pointed at his father. "Dad, you've never been good at taking your time."

Mid helped him to a sitting position. They could see that he had been lying on a spiral bound notebook. "Now, just stay here for a few minutes. Is your head spinning?"

"Not a bit. It was just a momentary thing. I'm good as new." His face brightened and he smiled.

Carol told the others, "All right. It looks as if no permanent damage has been done, thanks to the plush carpet here. Though that's going to need to be cleaned."

Louis said, "Oh, we can have it done." He scanned the room and then picked up the notebook. "What's this?"

Mid explained. "It's a history of the Lindblooms one of his cousins put together. It came in the mail this week."

"Yes," Oscar agreed. "Starts with my grandparents and follows their children's emigration to America. It includes pictures, newspaper stories, excerpts from letters. Fascinating stuff. I...I guess I was reading it."

Mid and Carol helped him back into the chair, and Mid insisted she wouldn't let him get up for a while. They would be fine. "You all go back to what you were doing," she shooed them away. "I'll keep a close watch on him."

Sam gave a nervous little laugh. "Okay. Now Grandpa, you get your head clear because we'll need your help with the Two-son Riddle. I'll come back in a little and tell you about the first clue."

Carol nodded. "And I'll return in half an hour to make sure you're okay. Louis, I need to talk with you about travel times."

Her schedule was not her primary interest. With the conspiracy among women established, Carol was turning to a second item on her agenda.

She had watched Louis become frustrated at the big dinner, not only because there was no immediate consensus that future family gatherings would be at the Overton Estate but also because his FACTH story was not judged the best. (Carol's was.) Neither development had surprised her, but she wanted Louis prepared for the future she foresaw.

Walking down the hall, she nodded back over her shoulder at their parents. "I'm afraid I don't like that."

"Oh, I think it's a one time thing. The blood rushes from your head. It's happened to me a few times."

"I've been quizzing Mom about this. He's had these little episodes, but she covers for him. When you took that trip with him out to Kansas this fall, how was he? As you know, I haven't been here since the spring."

They went into library and stood looking out the French windows at the snow-covered trees. "He was…fine. I mean, he was excited to see the places where he'd grown up, the little towns where the family found work in the Depression. It enabled him to keep the past together."

"He wasn't confused or forgetful?"

"Ah, well, that happens to anyone as you get on in years." He chuckled. "I did have a funny time explaining the 'film that's also a camera.'"

The "single-use camera" was popular at the time with tourists who didn't want to carry their own equipment, worried about removing and loading rolls of 35-millimeter film in unfamiliar places. The company put everything together into one package, which, after pictures were taken, would be mailed into a central office. The film was extracted there, prints developed, and the plastic camera case discarded.

Louis had bought one at the souvenir shop on the Kansas-Missouri border, promising his father he would record key scenes from his childhood. Oscar had been pleased with the results, but, now that Louis thought about it, once back in Fairfield, he had trouble keeping them in order and sometimes even misidentified places.

Carol admitted, "New technology can be confusing. Mark has had a hard time getting Dad to understand cellular telephones, despite his being a physicist. What I was thinking, though, is that it would be nice to organize some of Dad's memorabilia for him. You saw that family history he was studying. He could add to that from his own memories, maybe use those letters he has stashed away in his study."

"Dad does like to thumb through them now and then. He has even talked about trying to write a bit of his own autobiography; but he's not made much progress, as far as I know. I think he wanted us to think his story about Oswald the water tower climber was based on something he did as a boy, but I suspect it's a product of imagination more than memory."

"What if you decided to help him sort through his papers, at least getting them in some sort of chronological order? It would be a reason to go down to Fairfield on a semi-regular basis after the holidays and make sure they're doing okay."

"Ah, sort of surveillance, then."

"I do think it would be good if you could check in on them more often. Mom is so determined not to ask for help, but some things she says make me worry about them."

"Yes. All Dad will say is 'maybe I have lost half a step.'" He thought a minute. "I am in a position with the firm now that I can take more relaxed hours."

"You'd be doing the rest of us a big favor—well, two favors. Making sure they're all right and helping him with a project. Mom says that his band is getting fewer and fewer gigs these days. They're playing for an aging—and dwindling—population."

"Yes, whereas her clock business is steady if not growing. I'll think about this."

A few hours later, when Carol was checking on her parents, Sam came in with another Two-Son Riddle clue: a magazine ad for the movie, *The Three Amigos*. In this comedy three silent movie actors down on their luck are hired by a woman who believes they are the heroes they portray on the big screen. The three friends misunderstand her and think they will be shooting a film in Mexico, where they have actually been asked to rid a village of a villain.

"What we have so far is 'a wise man knows,'" explained Sam, showing the pictures of Einstein and a nose.

Mid wonders, "'A wise man knows'…what? Knows cowboys?"

"I haven't seen this movie," said Oscar. "Or any movie at the theatre—the crowds are too noisy. Now, on television," he said with enthusiasm, "there are some fine old films from the '40s. We had genuine stars then—Gable, Bogart, Tracy."

"Have you studied Spanish, Sam?" asked Carol.

"Well, not really, but I know what 'amigos' are—friends." Then his face lit up. "Of course, 'A wise man knows his friends.'"

Chapter Thirty-eight: Books

Next it was Curtis and Route 66. Carol found him stepping off the treadmill in the garage-become-gymnasium after finishing a 30-minute run-in-place. "Have you seen this?" She held up a book: *A Guidebook to Route 66.*

He wiped his hands on a towel. "Hmm. Looks interesting, but the cover is a bit old-fashioned, like it's from a Western movie in the time of stagecoaches."

"This is a reprint of the original, which came out in 1946. It was republished this spring, and I thought Louis might like it since his office—the Fruehauf building—is on the old road. But then I decided you would be more interested in it as a sign of the times—America returning to its own traditions at the end of the war."

"That's a point. It's probably one of the early signs of what the 50's would be like." He turned it over to view the back cover. He mused, "Of course, in Fairfield we grew up right on Route 66—well, pretty close to it. The old road ran right there on the other side of the railroad tracks."

Trains ran through a deep cut in the ridge parallel to Limestone Road, where the Lindblooms and other baby boomer families lived. People didn't see the trains, but the noise of their regular passing—as well as the ground shaking in some places—would sometimes bother new residents of the neighborhood.

Carol agreed. "Right. I didn't think much about it as a historic highway when I was a girl. But, over the last decade, as they began to decommission it in favor of interstate highways, I realized that we recognized it subconsciously as representing the possibility of travel, faraway worlds—'get your kicks on Route 66.'"

"Which you've certainly done in your military career."

She mused. "A new generation will soon be going farther and more often. The question is how many countries will get involved when we liberate Kuwait."

"I share your fear on that. I'm planning a reading of Aristophanes' *Lycistrata* when classes begin in January to raise awareness about the consequences of war."

"That's the one where the women tell the men there will be no more sex until the fighting stops, right? Now, there will be female warriors. I wonder if any of their men will kick them out of bed!"

He laughed. "I'll let you know, but society changes over time, doesn't it. A new need to carry traffic across the country in a post-war period of expansion led to limited-access highways, less incline on hills, broader curves—the end of Route 66."

"True, but I've also read there are groups coming together to preserve the old road, make it a historic landmark."

"It deserves a place in our cultural history. John Steinbeck called it 'The Mother Road' in *Grapes of Wrath* and it later inspired the television series in—when?— about 1960, I think. There's probably a larger body of work this reprint belongs to."

"Since I'm on the west coast and you're on the east, Route 66 is a place in memory for us more than a tangible thing. I guess that's why I thought you might find this book interesting. Well, and you are a teacher and a researcher. Maybe it will inspire a new phase for you."

He nodded. "One thing does interest me right away—the cover here is two men on a stage coach. More like the Pony Express than two eligible young bachelors in a Corvette exploring the country. But it's also interesting that there are no women in this picture, presumably no women anywhere in this rugged Western landscape."

A cactus, a distant mountain, and sagebrush were all that could be seen around the coach and the four horses out in front. This was Arizona or New Mexico before paved highways.

Carol admitted, "I guess Jack D. Rittenhouse, whoever he is, was after male readers."

"American men continued to mythologize the Wild West, the scene for radio *Gunsmoke* in the 50's and the television version in the 60's and 70's, plus hundreds of Western movies up to *Lonesome Dove*. So this archetypal image on a book cover might still get attention. But you do have a point: how are women part of this scene? There's not even a sign that the new school marm is coming from the East to insist 'there's been enough killing here'"

"I guess like Rosie the Riveter after the war, they're being told to quit their factory work, welcome home their returning husbands, have babies, and keep house."

"The question now is how might women react to a revival of Route 66? A new generation of feminists might see it as dangerously reactionary." He rubbed his chin. "This could be worth looking into. If there's a future for Route 66, how would the symbol have to change to pull together a much more complex society?"

Carol said, "Well, I'll leave that to your imagination. But I will say one thing: Mom might be an interesting person to talk to about this time. Remember, she came west in the 40's, a single woman on her own arriving in an alien land."

"That's right. She'd taken a position through the mail to work at the state health department. She was the pioneer of the family."

"As far as I know, she never took a factory job in New Jersey but worked in the medical field. And she went to Europe for a year or so with the Red Cross."

Curtis said, "There're still some blank spaces in her history, between her return from the war until she headed west. Has she ever talked to you about that?"

"Well, I know she went back to school sometime to certify as a medical technologist, and I always thought she worked in hospital labs. But how long that was, and where, I don't know." She snapped her fingers, as if struck by a sudden thought. "Something tells me she would enjoy talking about it. She's such a packrat that I bet she has photos, letters, newspaper clippings stashed away. If she got them out, you could organize them for her the next time you visit."

"I suppose I could ask her—assuming Dad is all right. I do wonder what inspired her to 'light out for the territory,' as Huck Finn calls it."

"You're a literary historian, what would a young professional woman see as her options at the end of WW II?"

He smiled. "I can tell you one thing: a renewed interest in major women writers wouldn't come until a decade or so later. The Victorian authors I admire—George Eliot, Charlotte Bronte, Elizabeth Gaskell—were slow to get back into the canon, being thought second-rate by the Moderns like Proust and Henry James. And, as you know, some of their novels appeared in installments, either separate parts or in magazine."

"Oh-ho, I think you just got on your hobby-horse."

As a literary scholar, Curtis argued against conventional opinion on serialization. Most academics believed the process of reading a novel over a year or more broke it into separate pieces that couldn't be held together by readers. So they insisted that students read single-volume editions where everything was between two covers.

To prove that parts published separately over time still come together into a coherent whole, Curtis had his own students read classic long works like Dickens' *Our Mutual Friend* and Trollope's Palliser series over the course of a semester or a year.

"I've already lectured you on the subject, to be sure," laughed Curtis. "But it does occur to me to wonder what kinds of stories were appearing in women's magazines in the later 40's, early 50's—*Ladies' Home Journal, McCall's, Good Housekeeping, Vogue.*"

"Well, I'll leave this project in your hands. In the meantime, I hope your Two-son Riddle isn't chauvinistic like this book. So far, it's all about wise men."

He chuckled. "Don't worry. I've got that covered."

And the next clue discovered by his daughter did suggest a broader range. "It's Mother Theresa," Mary Anne announced holding up a piece of paper that she'd found in a stack of lunch plates.

Ethel concluded, "A wise woman. But where's her nose?"

The other side of the paper featured a picture of a young girl playing with a 1950's erector set. "Toys?" offered Lucy.

"Builds," asserted Justin.

"Makes," insisted Christie.

"Ah," offered Sam, "'A wise man knows his friends, and a wise woman makes . . .'"

"We need to find the last clue to make sense of this. Let's go! Girls carriage house, boys main house, aunts and uncles outdoors!"

Chapter Thirty-nine: Tasks

After Oscar's fall Carol talked with her parents individually and together. She'd been questioning her mother regularly over the phone for some weeks after Mid had once hinted that Oscar was having "troubles." Before flying in for the Christmas holiday, Carol consulted a gerontologist friend she had worked with at the VA and did her own research on aging in contemporary journals. So, her announcement to her siblings and their spouses was the product of considerable reflection and represented a collation of information from many sources.

"Dad is showing signs of dementia," she announced matter-of-factly, then paused for immediate objections to this conclusion from her brothers.

But they looked blankly at her, and Suzanne was the first to speak. "Mom's been covering it up, I fear."

Louis turned to her, "You didn't tell me this."

"I did, but you haven't been listening. You're just like him, saying only that he's 'slowing down a bit.'"

Curtis worried. "Before today have there been major…incidents?"

"The signs of this kind of thing can be subtle," Anne noted. "We can conclude he's just getting older, when it could well be a more significant change."

Carol went on. "Yes, there are natural effects of aging—short-term memory loss, difficulty adapting to change, trouble following lines of thought. You could see it if you were watching him with the FACTH stories. When I quizzed him about some of them later, he was pretty confused."

Anne admitted, "He couldn't grasp why I was wandering around on rocks in Virginia. And he thought I'd been confronted by a mother bear."

"Some thing with my story," said Mark unhappily. "It wasn't clear who were the bees and who were the people."

Curtis said, "Now that you think about it, his reading and his television watching are all repeats—his favorite Edgar Rice Burroughs novels, movies from the 30's, old sitcoms. I thought this was just nostalgia, but it might be that he's narrowing his focus to what he knows well."

"What about his falling out of the chair?" asked Louis. "Is that connected to . . .to mental problems? My first thought was that it was a one-time thing, not part of a general condition."

"Unfortunately, it's happened a lot in the last six months," answered Carol. "At first Mom thought it was just carelessness. She couldn't decide which instance, when added to the others, constituted something she should tell us about. Since their house is carpeted, he's not been seriously hurt. But this does suggest an inability to focus, to remember where he is and what he's doing."

Suzanne admitted. "Mom told me he actually missed the chair in his study one day, sat right down on his coccyx. She had to take him to the doctor—mildly compressed vertebrae. It could have been much worst."

Carol said, "I don't think all this adds up to a dire situation yet, but it is wearing on Mom. Not only does she have to take care of herself as she ages, but she has to keep more careful track of him."

"He's still playing the saxophone, though, isn't he?" asked Louis. "He told me the Rockers of Age has a New Year's gig."

Carol answered, "I did some research about that. Musical memory can be much different than cognitive processing. His brain travels down the old paths but has trouble taking new directions." She looked at Curtis. "He's kind of like the cocker spaniels in your story. In a wide open field with many opportunities, he decides to go back to the known and familiar."

Louis nodded. "Rather than take the trips that Mom would like—back East, to Europe—he wanted to go back to his past, returning to his old haunts in Kansas." He paused. "But I have to admit he had some of his facts wrong about where and how he grew up."

"Mom says it's not quite so bad that she doesn't let him go out on his own. But in Fairfield he's traveling along familiar routes to known destinations. When they drove up here, she had to remind him about every turn."

Louis asked, "So, what shall we do? We're all together right now; it's the perfect opportunity. As I mentioned earlier, there are some very fine. . um…homes in the area."

"He won't want to leave Fairfield, let alone his house," Curtis pointed out. "And I think that's going too far too fast."

Suzanne said, "Carol, you look as if you have a plan."

"I do, and I've talked it over with Mom. We think we can start with a cleaning service that will come once a week. Take some over of the work she's been doing."

"That's a serious concession," admitted Anne. "Neither of them likes strangers coming into the house."

"I don't suppose we can hire a cook?" asked Mark.

"No, having someone there daily would set him off. But," she smiled. "But there is a caterer in town. Mom got

250

to know her because she had several clocks that needed repair."

Curtis said, "We all know Dad's very particular about what he eats. And I'm not sure both wouldn't balk at the expense. The Depression generation is very close with its money."

"That's why my Christmas present to them this year was a three-month gift subscription to Mrs. Farmer's Kitchen. Mom says she can give her the recipes she uses, and, in exchange for clock maintenance, her friend will bring her the meals Dad would be eating anyway. Each time there will be enough leftover for lunch at least."

Anne smiled. "It seems like you've thought of everything."

"I agree," said Louis. "But don't we need to get more medical supervision for both of them? Doctors don't make house calls anymore, as we all know."

"We'll have to employ a bit of a ruse there," explained Carol. "And I hope you'll go along with it. Mom is going to come home from a checkup next week and tell Dad she's been told she has to take it easy—some sort of joint pain, stiffness. Not debilitating, but something that requires home visits by a therapist."

"Ah, and that person's going to be checking Dad out at the same time?"

"Exactly. She's going to teach him how to help Mom with exercises—stretching, lifting small weights, that sort of thing. Knowing how Dad always likes to lead, I hope he'll be tricked into doing the exercises also. And he'll be asked to keep track of her activities—how many hours she's on her feet, her sleeping, all sorts of measurements."

Curtis pointed a finger at his sister. "I knew you were diabolical, but you've been like a spider weaving a web around all of us. And you've done this over the last few months without revealing a thing. You need to be watched yourself!"

She shrugged. "I guess she's confided in me—you know, the daughter. Still, we're all going to have to visit more frequently, perhaps coordinate with each other so not too much time passes without our finding out how they're doing."

Curtis smiled. "You haven't made a schedule have you?"

"Oh, this is just a rough sketch, a suggestion." She passed out a typed list of dates. "I've already made reservations to fly back at Easter. And I'd like to schedule fairly regular conference calls, so that we're all kept up to date."

Louis scanned the paper. "I see the first conversation is just five days away. Okay, I think we have a plan. Everyone else?"

Aware that there would have to be refinements to what she'd proposed, Carol was still satisfied that a framework had been established which would allow their parents to stay in their home for some time longer. When Abigail produced the final clue to Two-son Riddle, the family felt a resolution of more than this puzzle had been reached.

"Front side is easy," announced Justin. They all saw a red circle with a diagonal line through it. "Not, or none, or no."

The final clue took a bit longer to decipher: a chicken on a stage with trophies around it.

252

"A rooster? questioned Ben.

"Look again," chuckled Ethel. "That's a hen."

"So, a woman makes no chickens? Lays no eggs? Gets prizes for cackling?"

John squinted at the paper. "Those aren't just trophies, they're television Emmys."

"Ah-ha," proclaimed Lucy. "A wise man knows his friends; a wise woman makes no 'hen' 'Emmys'—no enemies!"

Chapter Forty: Triggers

Carol had begun her winning FACTH story this way. "I'd been at Harmon Motors to get my Jeep serviced. They were a bit slow that day, so after about an hour I began to wonder if I should step over to the diner for a cup of coffee--I missed the group of vets who gather there on Saturday mornings."

Louis interrupted. "Your car dealer's open on Saturday?"

"Saturday mornings. I know it's rare, but only one of the reasons I say this is the best car dealership in America. Anyway, all of a sudden this big guy--middle-aged, muscular, wearing all sorts of patriotic gear--pushed through the door, gun in hand."

"'Patriotic gear?' asked Mark, perhaps deliberately leading Carol.

"'Flags sown into his jacket, stars and stripes on pants, shoes, hat. There were slogans written all over his clothes, too, and he had tattoos in red, while, and blue on his gigantic arms. He was a big guy."

"Someone off his meds, sounds like to me," observed Curtis.

"You've never told us about that, Mom," claimed Marian. "Did you duck or what?"

"No time, and he was between me and the door. Not a happy situation, I assure you. I'd seen eyes like this before . . ." She trailed off a bit. Then resumed.

"There was no reason behind those eyes, just some blind fury. He didn't shout, but he had a huge voice--

stentorian, he was." Smiling at Curtis, she said, "There's a good word for you, English professor."

He shrugged. "I'll make a note of it, probably find occasions to use it more than once when classes start up in a few weeks."

"So, the man proclaimed that America was headed to hell, and he was going to put a stop to that, 'starting right here and now.' He pointed his 45 at the DMV lady, Alicia, who was frozen in her little window.'"

"How afraid were you?" asked Lucy, her eyes wide.

"Tell you the truth, I was mentally saying my farewells when Charles, the owner, strolls out of his office. It's not much more than a closet, just off the waiting room.'"

Carol loves this dealership: no frills; no high pressure salesmen; small inventory, a throwback to an older time in the midst of crowded, fast-paced, high-volume businesses sprouting up all around it. The interior has 1950s pine paneling--painted over in the '80s, though--the old wooden desk not right for the new electronic equipment, but Charles won't give it up. His daddy used to sit in the same spot. Gregory still comes in every day at age 91, as did his father when he retired. The grandfather founded the company after World War I.

"But Charles sees this guy and says, 'Willie, how you doing? Is your neighbor's old Aries holding up?' He acts like the guy is holding a peach or something, not a pistol. Walks right over to stand in front of him, between Willie and the DMV clerk. And the guy looks at him, not recognizing him, near as I can tell."

"Your chance to get away," notes Sam.

"Not yet. First, Clifford, the only salesman besides Charles, comes out of the repair area, and Charles turns to him. 'You know, it was this man's cousin, wasn't it, Cliff, the one who lived down behind the old lumber supply store, Martins', that we sold a truck to one time that he claimed could go faster in reverse than forward? Remember?"

"Cliff thought for a minute and said, 'That's right. Green Laramie SLT. Reliable as you'll find, though it did have its quirks."

"Charles turns to James, the office manager, who is standing in his window. 'That fella with the truck, he ever tell you about the Laramie going backwards so fast?' Still nothing from this Willie."

"James scratches his jaw a minute, then says, 'Tall guy, maybe six three, must have played some ball, if you ask me. Yeah, he did tell me about that truck. I told him, 'Bring it in, man; we'll check it out.'"

Louis said, "But the dealer or someone had already pushed an alarm in his office, right, and they were just stalling until the police got there?"

Carol hasn't mentioned yet that Charles is a veteran like his father and grandfather before him. She will explain that they'd all looked at guns that were looking at them.

"No, no alarm. Charles had just started chatting away the same way he does with anyone who comes in the shop or wanders by on the sidewalk. Asks them about their kin, children, neighbors, goings on in the community."

"So," asks Mark, again probably playing her straight man, "did he really sell cars to the gunman's family?"

"Not a one. He was flying by the seat of his pants, saying whatever seemed right for the moment. Had no idea who this was--at least at first--but read his name printed over the shirt pocket, like on an Army uniform. Willie's kin, it turns out, are nearly all gone from around there, and when they were alive they got their cars in an informal kind of barter system."

Curtis asked, "So this guy was local? Some people knew who he was?"

"Not really. We only learned later that he'd grown up in the county. No one could remember him exactly, even after he bought a car."

Louis shook his head. "Bought a car? You said you saw his eyes!"

"Yeah, but Charles saw something else, the way he held himself, for instance. Sensed a family resemblance, not to an individual but to folks Willie was related to. The stories Charles was telling were borrowed from men like him, maybe actual cousins or uncles or grandparents."

Sam protested, "I'm still not understanding why the guy didn't open up on everyone. Not that I would want anything to have happened to you, Aunt Carol!"

"Well, in his chatter Charles drew Willie into the community, gave him a place, a set of connections. He suggested his kin were county natives, part of local history. And Charles' assertions were close enough to what was true--or to what Willie might have liked to believe--that he started nodding, as if remembering those experiences, reliving them in his mind."

"Ah," offered Oscar. "Sort of like a spider weaving a web around a fly. When he got Willie all tied up, he turned him over to the authorities."

Carol shook her head. "After a bit, as he was listening to Charles, Willie tucked his gun into his belt. He leaned in, muttering 'Yeah, that's so,' or 'Now, I'd forgotten about that,' and 'Well, don't that beat all.' At one point he offered, 'Now, I remember that a bit differently. Wasn't a black bear, turns out, but a big black dog, dangerous, too, though in his own way.'"

"By now several repair persons had bought worksheets up to James, and he'd gone to totaling up bills. Clifford asked Alicia if those new DMV forms had come in. And Charles got around to mentioning he had some fine used cars out back, if Willie'd like to take a look. 'Seems to me you'd fit right in Dodge Charger I've got. It has some miles on it, but runs real smooth.'"

Suzanne was puzzled. "That's it? Walked out back. What did the rest of you do?"

"Me? Well, James told me my car was ready, so I stepped up to pay the bill."

"How much was it, by the way--tires and all?" asked Curtis. "Just curious."

"Don't have any idea. I just give James my credit card, and he rings it up."

"Louis exclaimed, "That's no way to run a business! But the guy's gun, Willie's, it was loaded? He drive off with it stashed in the Dodge Charger's glove compartment?"

"It was loaded, but he gave it to Charles. Asked him to put it in the office safe where nobody who shouldn't be handling a gun could get to it."

"Like a child...or a crazy person!" observed Oscar. "So, he left? Where'd he go?"

258

"Well, he and Charles settled on the price for the car, and when I left he was getting the license all straight."

"What did he have? A wad of bills stuffed in his pocket?"

"Not right then, but Charles figured he'd be able to pay once he got on the payroll."

"Oh, yeah, he got a job," said Curtis, slapping his forehead with one palm. "Of course! Why didn't I see that coming?"

"Charles found out Willie'd had experience in the motor pool, could work on trucks and older model cars."

Louis shook his head. "So, now there's a mechanic who should be in jail."

"Well, he'd be behind bars in St. Louis, I admit that. But there's a better lesson here, if you look for it."

There was silence for over half a minute. Then Mark observed with a smile, "But you're not going to tell us what it is, are you?

Epilogue: Removed

When Curtis came by my retirement apartment for his usual Wednesday lunch with me, he recounted an experience he and Anne had had visiting her cousins in Charleston. It started, he told me, with eleven-year-old Dora. "She frowned at me and asked, '"What am I to you?'"

"Ah, I said. "It's one of those second cousin once removed questions, isn't? Dora's dad is Anne's first cousin, so she's..."

He interrupted me. "Even though I've been in the South for forty years, I still can't keep complex relative categories straight; so I don't know what Dora is to me."

"We didn't worry about that sort of thing growing up in New Jersey," I admitted. "And they're even less important to Midwesterners."

"Well, I bring it up because you and me—mother and son—have just finished an account of the 1990 Christmas reunion in St. Louis. That extended weekend impressed upon me the importance of family relationships, and I'm refining my knowledge of terms. So, anyway, Anne, the Virginian, explained to Dora, 'Why, you're my first cousin once removed.' And she didn't like it."

"Why not?"

"'Removed'?" Dora complained. "'I don't want to be *removed*.' And I was struck by that, perhaps because I'm at that time of life when more and more of my contemporaries are facing the final remove."

"Well," I admitted, "you and I are going to have to go through your father's 'remove,' which came less than a year after that reunion with its FACTH stories, 'Route 66 to Palestine,' and your own 'Two-son Riddle.'"

"Yes, none of us were prepared for Dad's death. Thanks goodness you've hung around well into the next century to take on this project of writing a family history."

"Well, we're ready to start the final volume."

He corrected me. "'Final' only in so much as, when complete, it celebrates your first 100 years. I expect to start on the second set of five books twelve months from now."

He's a good boy and knows he's joking. All my doctors tell me my heart won't keep pumping forever. The mercy seems to be that it's likely to come to an abrupt stop rather than fall into a gradual decline. I told him, "You're going to tire of this project anyway. With my eyes getting so bad, I can't even help you organize photographs, letters, papers."

"Nonsense," he replied. "And my story of Dora will give you inspiration."

"In that case, please go on."

"Okay. So, my 'second cousin by marriage once removed' was still objecting to the term 'removed' when she got up from the kitchen table to put her plate in the sink. On the way past the trash container, she waved her hand, the lid lifted, and she dropped in her paper napkin."

"How did she do that?"

"Looked magical to me. But it's a light sensitive switch. When it's blocked, the lid comes up. Closes automatically, too, when the light hits it. But, when I asked her, Dora had another explanation: she said, 'I have...*the power*.'" He chuckled. "And I asked her if she had the power to conjure up another of the beignets her mother was serving us for breakfast."

"You wanted to take a picture of it with your phone, didn't you?" His son, Justin, is always sending pictures of the fancy food he and Olivia fix or have at restaurants; so he's taken to responding with pictures of his generally more ordinary dishes. This would impress John.

"I did wish I'd taken a picture. But then it occurred to me to take a picture of the empty plate with sugar dusting where the beignet had been. When I explained to Dora what I was doing, she giggled and told me to say it was a beignet 'once removed.' Immediately I saw it as the first in a series: a vegetarian lasagna, once removed; grilled salmon with fresh asparagus, once removed; etc. I would become a famous photographer; this time of life my would be my 'Once Removed' period."

This was a nice way to think of things, but the melancholy way he said it made me think he was also worrying about the process of his ongoing removal from an active professional life. As I had several decades ago, he now was finding himself removing to a smaller circle of friends in a gradual transition from large residence to smaller to small. Weeding out, throwing away, downsizing possessions and events. Not once removed, but a series of removals.

I asked, "Anne's uncle, Dora's grandfather, he's still alive, isn't he? One of the few in my generation still here."

"Yes, he's the last of four brothers who served in WWII. I always felt Bill suffered the most physically in that conflict. His oldest brother supplied troops pushing across Europe, and the next one down was an island-hopping Marine. They came home unscathed, but Bill had endured several tropical diseases requiring multiple infirmary visits and hospital stays. Much of his hearing was gone. When he finally came home, he'd lost so much weight and color that his mother failed to recognize him walking up the porch steps. Now," he said sadly," he is nearly 'removed' from his loved ones and this life."

"You were almost 'removed' that one time in Saigon, weren't you?"

An Army correspondent, Curtis had hopped a ride on a helicopter from Pleiku to Saigon. He later wrote a short piece about how he and his photographer decided to spend the few hours before curfew shopping the black market on Tu Do Street for electronic equipment. The three-wheel taxi driver they hired to get them back to MACV pedaled off into streets they'd never seen.

"I was lost," Curtis admitted. "But, as I've told you before, I finally realized that driver could have been as lost as I was. Many of the bicycle taxi drivers back then were refugees from the countryside or the North. He could have been recently arrived in Saigon, 'removed' from wherever the rest of his family were, learning the neighborhoods of a foreign city in order to stay alive."

I mused. "Now my grandchildren fly off to new cities in strange countries without blinking an eye. And the next generation will be even more at ease traveling around the globe. That Dora, for instance."

"She is a bright spirit," he agreed. "During our time there we went to visit her grandfather. She and I took a little walk through the grounds of his retirement center. Beside a small lake we found a white gazebo out on a dock. When the clouds darkened with an approaching storm the automatic lights came on. Dora squinted at them and asked, 'How did that happen?'"

"And you took credit, didn't you?" I laughed.

"You know me too well! I held up my hands and wiggled my fingers. 'I'm not saying,' I told you,' I said. 'But I might have…you know…*the power*.'"

"Did she like that?"

"She played right along, 'You're Dumbledore!' she claimed. We laughed, and I told her I can only use *the power* for good."

"Your cousin once-removed is special," I agreed.

"Actually, now she's more than that to us. Anne asked that evening if she had godparents. When her mother confirmed she didn't, Anne proposed we become her adopted godparents. And that's what we are—two adopted godparents not removed."

"Now that I've been in the South a few years, I have to admit there are good things about how people here see family. And how you're able to draw distant relatives close."

"Anne's the one with the gift—or *the power*—for that. But let me finish with one more chapter of our visit in Charleston. Dora was playing Kick the Can with her friends that evening. We could hear them from time to time calling, laughing, running. Us old folks were reminiscing at the kitchen table, helping with the clean-up after dinner. When I opened the trash at one point—or it opened for me—the smell of pencil shavings wafted up to greet me. She'd sharpened a couple of dozen for school. I felt like I was in kindergarten again."

I laughed. "Brings it back, doesn't it? Smells have always done that for me, though my nose, like lots of there things, doesn't work as well as it used to."

"Well, I confessed that I thought I'd put kindergarten well behind me, but I still had to make a few of the usual jokes—like we had no pencils or crayons back then. We had to draw with our fingers in the dirt floor."

"And walk barefoot in the snow," I agreed "No shoes, no books, no lunch boxes. Oh, your dad and I made it hard for you."

He paused and looked off into the distance. "I was laughing, but, at the same time, my mind had somehow filled with gloomy thoughts, made more so by the approach of a thunderstorm. I heard the wind swishing through the Spanish moss, and I could smell a coming storm. I worried about my adopted goddaughter outside."

"We want *the power* to protect our children more than anything."

"We do, indeed, especially, it seems to me, as we get older. Thinking about Dora and her grandfather, the WW II veteran, I especially wanted to be able to help him remove from this world with little suffering. I wanted to restore his memory so that every delightful new thing Dora said or did would stay with him even as he slipped away. And for a moment I envisioned Dora taking her grandfather's hand and gently ushering him into the everlasting, wherever it will be."

I patted his hand. "I'm sure you helped both of them in your visit."

He sighed. "I hope so, but I was helped more myself in the end. While I was fantasizing, Dora burst through the patio doors. I was relieved she had come in before the storm hit because at the same moment she appeared a bolt of lightening split the darkness, and the lights went out. Her dad clicked on his cell phone light, so we could all see. And then Dora pointed at me. 'Mr. Godparent—do the lights.'"

"Uh-oh, put you on the spot, didn't she?"

"She most certainly did. So, hoping to stall and get lucky, I stretched his fingers, preparing for a wave of magic. And, miracle of miracles, the lights came back on. She laughed, 'You did it again, Dumbledore!'"

"I've always thought you were magic," I chuckled. "Or at least special"

"I can't take the credit, but I did accept the reward. Dora gave me a quick hug and returned to that earlier project of sharpening pencils. So I asked her, 'Say, what happens to all the wood that used to be at the end of your pencils—you know, around the lead?'"

"Oh, any mom can tell you that," I insisted. The shavings go into blue jean pockets, lunch boxes, shoes.

And then children carry them home to scatter all around the house."

He chuckled. "Good answer, but Dora had a better one. She said, 'Oh, Mr. Married to my Dad's First Cousin, that's simple: those shavings have simply been . . ."once removed!"'"

I laughed, but not as hard or as enthusiastically as Curtis said he did.

"The laughs," he explained, "spread through the group until everyone was sharing the joy. Dora looked at all us adults, a bit surprised by the success of her joke. And then said, 'Well, I do have…you know, *the power*.'"

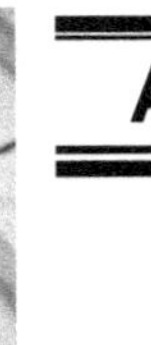

About the Author

Michael Lund.

A native of Rolla, Missouri, Michael Lund is the author of numerous scholarly publications on the Victorian novel, two collections of short stories--How to Not Tell a War Story (2012) and Eating With Veterans (2015)--and a number of novels inspired by The Mother Road, including Route 66 to Vietnam: A Draftee's Story (2004), Growing up on Route 66 (1999), and Route 66 Looking-Glass (2014). Professor Emeritus of English at Longwood University in Virginia, he teaches part-time and conducts writing workshops with Home and Abroad, a free writing instruction program for veterans, active-duty military, and families hosted by Longwood University's Department of English and Modern Languages.

Michael Lund's short story, "Old Soldier," is included the anthology, On the Back of a Motorbike, just published by Literary Concepts, available in paperback and in

Michael Lund's short story "Left-hearted" was awarded second finalist in the COL. DARRON L. WRIGHT AWARD sponsored by Line of Advance, a curated platform for the best in writing and other visual arts from American military veterans.